DAWN LEE
MCKENNA
&
AXEL
BLACKWELL

# DEAD AND GONE

## A STILL WATERS SUSPENSE NOVEL— BOOK 3

2019

A SWEET TEA PRESS PUBLICATION
First published in the United States by Sweet Tea Press
©2018 Dawn Lee McKenna & Axel Blackwell. All rights reserved.

Edited by Debbie Maxwell Allen

Cover by Shayne Rutherford
wickedgoodbookcovers.com

Interior Design by Colleen Sheehan
ampersandbookinteriors.com

ISBN: 978-0-9986669-6-9

*For Frank and Lucy*
*with gratitude and love*
*—**Dawn Lee***


*&*


*For Jo, always*
*—**Axel***

# AUTHORS' NOTE

IN OCTOBER, 2018, Hurricane Michael devastated the Florida Panhandle, particularly Gulf and Bay Counties.

I (Dawn Lee) went down to the Panhandle about a week after the hurricane. The destruction was tragic. My first thought was "Andrew". A native Floridian, I have always loved hurricanes and tropical storms, as many of my friends and family did. Crackers don't evacuate, they nail plywood over the windows and have a potluck. This isn't because Floridians are reckless; it's because 99% of the hurricanes we've experienced, at least in my lifetime, knock down tree limbs and power lines but seldom result in tragedy. That changed with Hurricane Andrew in 1993.

I cannot overstate the shocking sights that greeted me that October. Houses moved across the street. Dozens and dozens of pelicans dead on the bridge to St. George Island. Roads with enormous craggy chunks of asphalt sticking straight up in the air, as though there'd been an earthquake. One of my favorite restaurants, gone without a trace. Not a trace.

But the worst damage that I saw along the coast (Michael destroyed whole communities and hundreds of acres of trees way far inland, too) was in Panama City, Panama City Beach, Mexico Beach and Port St. Joe.

The Port St. Joe Marina, where Evan and Sarah live (yes, it is real, like almost all of the locations in the books), was decimated. Every boat was sunk to some degree. One gentleman, recently widowed, was living on his boat with his cat. He and the cat survived, their home did not.

After the hurricane, Axel and I talked at length about how to approach the realities of Hurricane Michael in a fictional series that was set right in the middle of Michael's destruction. We agreed that it had to be addressed; anything else would be disrespectful to the people who have been so enormously affected by the storm.

But we also agreed that we would not write a book in this series *about* the storm. That would be equally disrespectful, because it is not something that should be used as entertainment. Even though *Landfall*, the fourth book in my *Forgotten Coast Florida Suspense* series was all about a hurricane, it was based on a storm from the

1980s, a storm that did not result in great loss of life, or the disappearance of an entire town.

We decided that one of the books would be set after the hurricane, and address the damage, the changes to Port St. Joe, and how it affects our characters, without actually writing about the storm. We hope to honor the residents of the Panhandle, particularly Port St. Joe, by writing about the enormous outpouring of help to the area, the heroism of regular people, and the tenacity, strength, faith and generosity that has been shown every single day since the hurricane.

This book was already half-finished at the time of the storm, and the plot of the fourth book, Dead Wrong, really doesn't allow for the inclusion of Hurricane Michael. So, that will be done in the fifth book, which is as yet untitled.

We hope that the people of Gulf, Bay and Franklin County will feel counted, remembered, and acknowledged by our efforts.

Meanwhile, if you would like to support the people of the area, many of whom are still homeless, many of whom have lost every material thing, I set up and funded a 501c3 non-profit called The UnForgotten Coast Fund, which is dedicated to granting microloans to individuals, families and small businesses. These loans, which carry no interest or deadline for reimbursement, are meant to cover expenses that are not being met by insurance or government assistance, things that will enable people to get back to work or back into their homes.

If you'd like to contribute, you can do so via the non-profit's Facebook page at:

FB.COM/PAGES/CATEGORY/NONPROFIT-ORGA-NIZATION/THE-UNFORGOTTEN-COAST-FUND-PAGE-191407815093891/.

Even if you can't help financially, please pray for guidance and wisdom for the non-profit, and for healing, strength and new life for the people of the Florida Panhandle.

# ONE

A NARROW SHAFT of afternoon sunlight sliced through the otherwise darkened stateroom. Evan pressed his back into the bulkhead, a thin scrim of sweat sticking the cotton of his shirt to his skin. He flared his nostrils, breathing deeply and deliberately, silently. The portholes were shut, and he felt a small bead of perspiration drop to his forehead from his slightly damp black hair.

Somewhere, deeper within his boat, the killer waited, perhaps as yet unaware of Evan's presence. A single tiny drop of blood glimmered bright red in the gloom, just beyond the threshold. It was way too late to save a life, but he might still catch the killer in the act.

Outside, ripples lapped at the starboard hull as some weekend mariner, oblivious to the drama playing out just yards away, maneuvered his vessel out of the marina, apparently unconcerned by the fact that they were in a no wake zone. An annoyance for another day; a killer was at hand.

Reflected ripples danced lazily across the porthole on the starboard side of the master stateroom. On the port side, the dock lines groaned, and the fenders creaked against the dock. Evan strained his ears, searching for the faintest hint of movement beyond the door. But within his walls, all was still.

Evan's cell phone weighed against his chest in the pocket of his button-down shirt. He tried to remember if he had silenced it. His green eyes sparked with realization, and the thin white scar that ran from his lower lip to his chin shone more brightly than usual against his deeply-tanned skin as he set his jaw.

Evan's history with the perpetrator told him that he was waiting just as silently, just as aware of Evan as Evan was of him. Waiting just as patiently; actually, probably more so. The cold killer knew Evan was there, that he was waiting him out, and that he was alone.

It probably didn't matter whether he'd silenced his ringer; Evan probably wasn't being as stealthy as he thought he was, anyway. If he had failed to silence it, well then it was what it was. If a call or text came in at just the wrong moment, it would give away his position for sure, but so would fidgeting for his phone in this dim light, with his quarry so close at hand.

He wanted a cigarette and that irritated him, made him even angrier at the killer.

He dismissed thoughts of the cigarettes in his back pants pocket, or the phone in his right breast pocket. He focused instead on the weapon concealed beneath the opposite breast of his jacket. He slipped his fingers around its smooth grip, simultaneously toeing the state-room door. He knew his boat well, knew that the hinges would utter not the slightest squeak, but still he hesitated.

The motion of Evan's boat on the marina's calm water was barely perceptible. Out on the bay, motors rumbled, their lower tones carried across the distance under the water's surface. Other, closer sounds marked time, creak-ing, ticking, groaning in organic orchestration. Evan waited until these noises peaked, to cover any sound he might make in his approach.

He applied pressure to the door with his toe, gripping his weapon and slowly drawing it from his suit coat. As the door swung wider, the sight it revealed might have stopped a greener detective in his tracks. The brutal vio-lence of the scene would likely elicit some gagging, or at least a gasp, from the average civilian, or a cop with a weaker constitution. But Evan had a strong stomach, and from recent experience he'd known what to expect, had steeled himself against it.

Even so, the severed head, the white gleam of de-fleshed bone, the string of unraveling entrails assault-ed his sensibilities. He wasn't sure if it was the raw vio-lence of it, or simply the fact that it was on his gleaming hardwood sole.

His revulsion was instantly met by one of his training officer's slogans, back in the day: lean into it. Lean into the emotions. Evan raised his weapon, its stubby muzzle gleaming bright red like the drops of blood, then rushed through the door, slapping the light switch with his other hand. He swept the room with his weapon in a fast, smooth arc. Half-way through the sweep the killer appeared. Evan froze the second his crosshairs centered on his target.

The killer froze as well, crouched on Evan's bed, eyes wide with either alarm or defiance. Evan didn't have time to determine which, nor did he have much interest in knowing. Unlike some cops, he had no fascination with the mind of a killer; he knew only what he had to know to beat one, and to survive doing it. Three mutilated bodies in the space of four weeks. He really didn't need any additional insight into the killer's psyche.

There was a singular moment of tensed muscles and intense silence, then Evan triggered his air horn. The silence of the afternoon disintegrated in a painfully loud reverberation. The close quarters magnified the sound to the point that Evan almost regretted his choice of weapon. Or he might have, if the effect hadn't been so primally satisfying.

Plutes shot straight upwards, as if he had inadvertently tried to cross a geyser at just the wrong moment, his eyes nearly as wide as Evan's. Then he hit the floor, all four legs already running, and running in four different directions.

His back end spun almost level with his front end, his toenails fighting for purchase on the slick wood sole, as he flew past Evan and through the stateroom door.

"Go ahead and run, you jerk!" Evan yelled after him. "I left a little gift on *your* pillow, too!"

Half a moment later, he heard the short yowl. Predictably, Plutes had run for his overpriced kitty cubby. It had been just big enough for three overfilled water balloons.

Evan allowed a small smile of satisfaction. The cat had disassembled one too many mice on his 600-thread count, organic, brushed Egyptian cotton pillowcases.

After Plutes' vanishing act, with the echoes of the air horn still screaming through his head, Evan assembled his sanitation supplies. He wished the cat's messes disappeared as readily as the cat himself did. But such was not his luck. He'd gone topside to the sun deck for a cigarette, then pulled on a pair of Latex gloves and gotten to work.

He had a strong stomach, but it didn't make the filth on his pillow any easier to take. It would have been fine on anyone else's pillow, but Evan's OCD cleanliness was screaming at him from within.

For the third time that month, he considered just putting the mattress, and the cat, on Craigslist. But he was too broke to get rid of the mattress, and too stubborn to get rid of the cat. He wouldn't be tormented into doing anything, no matter how pleasant the prospect might be.

On his way back down the dock, he failed to notice the backward glances of two young women who passed him going the other way. The looks weren't a rare occurrence; Evan was a youthful forty, with a perennial tan, piercing green eyes, and black hair that shone like it was lit from underneath. It wasn't rare for him to miss the attention, either. He knew women found him attractive; but his lack of both interest and social awareness made that easy for him to forget.

Once back on board his 45-foot, 1986 Chris-Craft Corinthian, he pulled another pair of latex gloves out of his pocket and slipped them on before plucking the various bits of mouse morsel off the bed linens and dropping them into a trash bag. He peeled the case off his pillow, thanked God for waterproof pillow protectors, and dropped the linens into the washing machine, then set to work scrubbing his beloved hardwood sole with a rag and a bottle of cleaner. By the time he'd finished cleaning up the blood and gore, even God would have needed a can of luminol to find it.

He carried the whole mess down to the dumpster at the end of his dock, and had just leaned against a palm to light a cigarette when Sarah appeared from the back of the Dockside Grill, the restaurant belonging to the Port St. Joe Marina.

Sarah the Muffin Girl, as Evan still thought of her sometimes. He'd gotten to know her a bit better over the last few months, but she still delivered muffins and the Sunday paper to every boat, courtesy of the marina. At a purported seventeen, she was a curious mixture of punk and rockabilly, grit and fragility, and weighed just a couple more pounds than Plutes.

She stopped as she reached Evan, and squinted through the sun at him from beneath per black pixie cut.

"Hey," she said.

"Hey." Evan blew a mouthful of smoke in the other direction.

"I thought you said you were quitting." She perched a delicate, tanned hand on her sharp little hip.

"I quit every day," he said, as he ground out the cigarette then popped the butt into the trash. "Where've you been? I was starting to worry about you."

"Aw. Just some family stuff, plus I'm studying. I'm trying to get into Gulf Coast State."

"Everything okay with your family?" Evan asked, his radar beeping. Sarah's family consisted of a bunch of notorious meth cookers and dealers. Sarah had little contact with them.

"Yeah, it's cool. Just some stuff with my mom," she answered.

She had turned to look down the dock, and he knew she was evading him. He let it go.

"Gulf Coast State, huh?" The school was a large community college in Panama City. It had a good reputation. "Have you figured out what you want to study yet?"

She scratched at one bony arm that sported an assembly of silver bangles and black hair ties. He had no idea what she tied with them, as her hair wasn't much longer than his.

"I'm still thinking nursing," she said, and she almost winced, like she expected him to think that was either funny or stupid.

"Nursing, teaching kindergarten; you seem well-suited for either one."

She did. She slipped scripture quotes into his newspapers and Tupperware containers of soup onto his sun deck. As incongruous as it might seem, from the mire of dysfunction and felony that was her family had crawled a born nurturer.

"I was thinking that if I become a teacher, I'm kind of stuck in one place, you know? But travel nursing is a thing, and that would be kind of cool," she said, her shield lowered. "I could sail from one job to the other, like all up and down the Gulf Coast. Travel nurses make a lot more money, too, and I can take time off between jobs if I feel like it."

"You've put some research into this," Evan said. He felt a twinge, a little tickling in his chest, at the thought of her one day leaving. He didn't much care for change.

"Yeah." That tensing again, like she thought she might have to dig her heels in.

"Do it. You have to learn to sail first," he reminded. "And get a seaworthy boat."

"Yeah, both of those things would probably be helpful," she agreed.

The marina paid Sarah with a small wage as well as a roof of sorts; she lived on a late seventies Hunter 25 that someone had abandoned. It had no shower and only the bare minimum of a galley, but she got two meals a day at the Dockside Grill, and showered in the clean facilities across from the office, used by a lot of boaters that came through. At her age, Evan would have killed for her situation.

Evan had been through nine foster homes before being adopted by Mike and Frances Caldwell when he was thirteen. At seventeen, his days had been filled with school and surfing, his nights with revising his college entrance essays and selling Mrs. Fields cookies at the Dadeland Mall.

With the hindsight afforded a forty-two-year-old man, Evan thought a low-wage, low-responsibility existence on a small sailboat might have done him more good than trying to shake the residue of the foster system with an education and a high-paying job. He'd veered from his plan and become a cop after graduating instead of a civil attorney, but that was the way things shook out.

"What was your major?" Sarah asked him.

"Psychology," he answered dryly. "Ironically."

"I saw you and Plutes comin' in from surfing yesterday," Sarah said.

"Yeah."

It was only surfing because Evan called it that. There was no surfing in Port St. Joe, so Evan liked to substitute taking out the runabout. By some perverted twist of fate, it happened that Plutes liked to surf, too. At least the black mamba had *some* sense. Not that Evan was in any danger of becoming one of those inexplicable cat people or anything. It just made being stuck with the cat a tad more palatable.

"I would have taken you out but you weren't around."

"You guys have fun?" she asked.

"Marginally," Evan answered. "I've gotta rework the whole backpack set-up. That fatass gives me a crick in my neck."

"You know what's really interesting about you?" she asked, squinting at him like a therapist.

"No, but I'm sure that's a euphemism," he answered with a curled lip.

"It probably is, but I don't know what that word means," she said. "But what's interesting is that you don't even realize you like that cat."

"The mouths of babes and all that," Evan replied.

She opened her mouth to answer but Evan felt the buzz of his cell phone vibrating against his chest. He pulled it from the pocket of his white button-down shirt and checked the screen. When it told him the call was from George Dinkelman, he considered answering it with his air horn.

"Let me guess," Sarah said, noticing his change in demeanor, "It's either the dentist or a crazy ex."

"I wish," Evan muttered, "It's Dinkelman."

"The shrubbery guy?" Sarah asked, with a grin.

Evan nodded, sighing. His Sunday, his one day off in two weeks, was blown. "I'll see you later, kid."

Sarah flashed him a peace sign and her little Tinkerbell smile, and Evan turned and headed back down the pier.

The phone buzzed again in his hand. He tapped the little green icon to accept the call that he knew would scuttle whatever plans he may have had for the rest of his Sunday afternoon.

# TWO

HALF AN HOUR later, Evan found himself piloting his Pilot through a freshly constructed housing development known as Seaview Cove. The Cove was one of Gulf County's newer residential areas, and it was about to become the newest neighborhood in Port St. Joe – if, that was, the county commissioners and the PSJ city council had their way.

The tidy little nest of homes lay on a tract of county land that snuggled right up against the city limits. The city wanted the tax revenue the new homes promised, and the county didn't want to spend the money required to upgrade their infrastructure to properly support the influx of residents.

The speed with which the homes in Seaview Cove had popped up, and the uniformity of their architecture, prompted some of the more seasoned Port St. Joe residents to refer to them as mushrooms. Evan didn't have any opinion, one way or the other, about the mushrooms, or about the development's civic oversight, but he had had quite enough of the developer himself.

George Dinkelman was a transplant from…somewhere. Evan never had gotten a straight story about the man's origin. He spoke with a gruff British accent he certainly hadn't been born with, and affected several other idiosyncrasies intended to indicate sophistication and superiority. The man's belly and broad nose could only be described as Shrek-like, and though he stood almost six feet tall, his proportions gave him a squat appearance.

Evan wound through roads that had been unnecessarily twisted, apparently to give the development a more organic feel and to offset the unimaginative architecture. After several minutes, the occupied homes with pristinely constructed landscapes gave way to freshly-painted, vacant houses. These were followed by nearly completed structures settled into dirt lots.

As Evan ventured deeper into The Cove, he saw fleets of dusty wheelbarrows laying upside-down in neat lines, locked together with heavy chain. Juvenile palm trees, their root balls tied up in burlap, huddled like aberrant jungle teepees. These, also, had been secured with heavy chains and padlocks.

Evan groaned.

It was trees that had started this whole mess. The developer had ordered several truckloads of exotic trees and bushes to adorn the lots. As soon as they had arrived, someone began stealing them. A few of the trees had even been dug up and stolen after the landscapers had planted them. Dinkelman was convinced the thieves were from Happy Garden, what he described as a bottom-of-the-barrel landscaping company out of Panama City, and insisted Evan send detectives over to stake out their operation. Evan had declined, mainly because Panama City was out of his jurisdiction, but also because he didn't feel like it.

Dinkelman hired a security guard to do plant patrol, but the maze-like layout of the development made it nearly impossible for one man to secure. Evan had asked his deputies to roll through the development as often as feasible, and had coordinated with the Port St. Joe Police Department to get their help with patrols as well, but the trees continued to sneak off in the night.

Dinkelman had purchased hundreds of cable-lock alarms, which flashed and emitted a siren when triggered. These were intended for display model electronics at retail outlet stores, but Dinkelman had attached one to every tree he considered valuable.

Eventually, one of these alarms triggered at the same time a PSJ patrol was cruising the development. The responding officer caught sight of a young man in a hoody running down the street with something called a Japanese Raisin Tree in a wheelbarrow. The officer gave chase and managed to recover the tree, and the wheelbarrow, but the hoodie got away. Since that incident, only a few smaller bushes had disappeared.

Evan eventually reached the far back end of the development where, after a final curve, the road ended in a cul-de-sac. Here, the bright yellow pine skeletons of several houses patiently waited for their bones to be dressed in a more presentable fashion. George Dinkelman also waited, neither patiently nor fashionably.

Dinkelman certainly had wealth and influence, evidenced by the speed with which he managed to obtain building permits or other favors from city and county officials. And the speed with which he demanded results. Evan imagined it was that wealth and power that allowed him to get away with dressing the way he did. Today, it was rumpled trousers of an un-named color that Evan could only imagine having been the result of some egregious error at the dye factory. Either that, or haute couture. Above these, he wore a sweater which, Evan deduced, must have been the non-festive, Neanderthallic ancestor from which ugly Christmas sweaters had evolved.

The man leaned, with arms folded over his formidable gut, hands jammed into his armpits, against his silver Mercedes. The scowl he wore pinched his face into creases, pulling his shrubbery-like eyebrows together and thrusting his nose into the world ahead of him as if it were the pick with which he hammered his way through life.

Evan pulled his Pilot to the curb a few yards from Dinkelman and stepped out. On the deserted street, under the bright Florida sun, with animosity radiating from the developer, Evan almost felt like he was walking into the climax of a Spaghetti Western. He had to stop himself from checking the sky for buzzards.

"Mr. Dinkelman," he said warily. "What can I help you with?"

Dinkelman glowered without speaking. His lower jaw jutted, his brow twitched, and a shudder ran through him. He huffed a breath out through his nose and demanded, "Do you not see it?" He swung an arm to the side and said, "The garbage! They are using my estates as a garbage dump!"

On one of the dirt lots, two Bud Light six-packs lay overturned. Their empty bottles littered the ground around them like dead mosquitos under a bug zapper.

"And look what they have done to my pavement!"

"Doughnuts." Evan said, noting the swirls and curli-cues of rubber burned into the roadway.

"Dough...Doh!" Dinkelman blustered. "You think this is funny, Caldwell? I didn't call you here to laugh at me. You have a job to do! Why aren't you doing it?"

Evan was still mentally testing all of the first answers that came to mind when the man saved him the trouble of a civil response by going on.

"Do you have any idea how much I pay just in prop-erty taxes on this land? That's money, coming out of my pocket and going into your pocket," Dinkelman thrust a stubby finger at Evan, as his face reddened, "for the express purpose of you making sure that I don't have to deal with this…" he waved his arm at the marks on the pavement, then at the beer bottles.

Evan guessed the developer had worked something out that allowed him to pay far less property tax per dollar of assessed value than the average Gulf County resident, but he decided to let that lie for now. He was determined not to become the politician his current title suggested, but tact had always been his default. He figured he could manage just a bit now, if only to keep this meeting as short as possible. In any case, if the man's blood pressure climbed any higher, he might blow an embolism, which wouldn't hurt Evan's feelings too much, but would definitely cut even further into his plan for the evening which was, as usual, to visit his wife.

"Mr. Dinkelman, I'm sorry about this mess. I can empathize with the aggravation you're feeling. I believe you will find that most of the people out here tend to be respectful, reasonable folks," Evan said, mustering as much sincerity as he could. "Of course, there are always one or two…"

"Well, I don't give a damn if it's two or two-hundred and twenty-two!" Dinkelman shouted. "Keep them the hell out of my development!" He took a step forward, his finger inching closer to Evan's chest. Evan tensed, simultaneously hoping and dreading that the man might actually poke him.

"Catch them! Arrest them! Do your job!" Dinkelman's face had gone almost purple, and tiny beads of sweat twinkled like glitter on his otherwise colorless forehead.

"Mr. Dinkelman-" Evan started.

"Don't 'Mister Dinkelman,' me!" He was shouting now, and up on his tiptoes, assumably so he'd be taller than Evan, though they were the same height.

"This has been going on way too long. First it was the trees, now it's garbage and vandalism. What will it be next? Huh? Burglaries? Arson? Why, I feel I must count the houses every time I drive in here, just to make sure someone hasn't run off with one overnight!"

By this point, the man's face was only inches from Evan's, but the finger remained a safe distance from his chest. This gave Evan a bit of hope for his evening. Dinkelman had obviously learned from their last encounter not to touch the sheriff. It was a lesson Evan didn't expect him to forget. If he could learn that, maybe, given enough time and patient instruction, he might learn to speak without spraying.

"George!" Evan said, not at volume, but with sufficient force to shut the man up and startle him back a pace. "First of all, remember what I said about the two-foot rule. I assure you that I downplayed the repercussions."

This evoked a bit more startle and another half-pace retreat from Dinkelman.

"Now, I have a very important appointment this afternoon that I've already postponed on your account. I'm happy to leave, at any moment, if you continue giving me reason."

Evan watched Dinkelman's jaw tighten, the muscles at its corners bulging. He lowered his head, just a tick, like a bull getting ready to charge, and his fists balled. But he also dropped his heels and his finger.

Evan nodded, then continued, "Now, due to the issues you've been having, this little development is the most heavily patrolled patch of ground in the entire county. If you like, you can come down to the station and I will show you the patrol logs." Dinkelman tried to interrupt, but Evan stopped him with a gesture and continued. "We have even had two of the homeowners call to complain about all the cops driving up and down the roads."

"It obviously hasn't done any good, has it?" Dinkelman blurted, gesturing again to the beer bottles, all twelve of them.

"Now you're just being obtuse. We stopped the tree thieves, didn't we?" Evan asked. "Have you had anymore stolen landscaping?"

"Tree thieves!" Dinkelman looked to the side and huffed out a snort. "I know you think it's funny. I know you are all laughing about it back at the station. This is what I get for trying to bring beauty into this ugly little corner of the world."

Evan was a newcomer, having moved to Port St. Joe only several months ago, but he took offense to the slight nonetheless. Port St. Joe might be worlds away from Miami or even Cocoa Beach, and he often felt like a stranger in a strange land, but no one could call the place ugly.

Evan watched some of the wind go out of Dinkelman's sails. His face cooled to something that resembled flesh color.

"We lost nearly ten-thousand dollars-worth of exotic horticulture," Dinkelman said more evenly. Evan noticed the effort it took. "I've had to settle for native plants for almost all the landscaping here because I couldn't afford to lose any more of the better species. I know you think this is all about me, but it's the homeowners who suffer. This place could have been beautiful, but now it's just another piece of backwater Florida." Dinkelman lowered his head a bit and let it shake from side to side.

"Look, George," Evan said, sighing. "I can't assign more patrols out here than I already have. It wouldn't be fair to the rest of the county. What is it, specifically, that you want me to do for you?"

Dinkelman looked up, eyes blinking in surprise. "Catch the bastards! Find out who is responsible and put them in jail. Look! Evidence!" He waved his arms at the tire tracks and the bottles. "Do the… the police thing! Call your CSI team. Get fingerprints from the bottles and… and DNA! Make plaster casts of the tire tracks and check them through your data base!"

Evan reigned in another sigh. "It doesn't work that way, George."

"Listen, Sheriff. I know you think this isn't worth your time, but I'm telling you, you let these guys get away with little things, and it'll just get worse. It always does. They don't stop unless you stop them. As soon as I am done with you, I'll be on the phone with Councilman Quillen. I guarantee you he will take me seriously. Quillen has a good head on his shoulders, understands the priorities in situations like these."

"Look," Evan said, now trying for a conciliatory tone, "I'm not sending a crime scene tech out here on a Sunday afternoon to fingerprint beer bottles." He again had to silence Dinkelman's attempt to interrupt before continuing. "But here's what I'll do. Set them inside your little trailer office thing there and I will send a tech out tomorrow morning, first thing. He can collect any prints there might be and run them. Maybe we'll get a hit."

"Monday!" Dinkelman barked. "What if he comes back tonight?"

"Then there will be more evidence to collect," Evan said. "Tell you what, how about I give you a roll of yellow police-line tape. If anything new shows up between now and then, put the tape around it to protect the evidence and we'll collect it tomorrow morning."

Dinkelman glowered, likely trying to determine whether Evan intended the gesture sincerely, or as ridicule. It was mainly the latter, but Evan didn't like Dinkelman enough to tell him that.

He reached into his Pilot to retrieve the tape, hoping Dinkelman didn't guess the truth. He was already running late for his nightly chat with Hannah and risked missing visiting hours completely. Either way, as Evan dropped the roll into Dinkelman's hands, he decided the conversation was over. For today at least. The sun was almost to the horizon and most of the lighter palette was out of the sky, giving way to the deeper shades a coastal sunset.

As Evan pulled out of the development and onto the county road, he lit a cigarette he would have tripped an elderly woman for. Without his consent, his brain said something about the fact that, now that Dinkelman was behind him, he wouldn't have to listen to anybody for the rest of the evening.

A sickening swirl looped through his stomach at the unbidden thought. No, Hannah wouldn't be subjecting him to any conversation tonight.

Sunset Bay, lauded as the best assisted living facility in Florida, looked more like one of Dinkelman's creations than a place where the infirm, the dementia-damaged and the comatose might reside. It was the reason he'd sold everything he'd owned and come here from Cocoa Beach, where he'd been employed by the Brevard County Sheriff's Office for several years. He spent every spare dime on the place, and most of the ones he couldn't spare, too.

It was close to seven by the time Evan made his way down the main hall of the East Wing, and most of the residents were in bed. The tastefully-decorated corridor was quiet, even his footsteps softened by the well-padded tile floor.

As he started to pass the nurse's station, a woman in her twenties, with dark, blunt-cut hair and pink scrubs, stood up to look over the counter. Ellie. He liked her a lot. He liked all of the staff, but she stuck out as one of the particularly committed.

"Hi, Mr. Caldwell. Sheriff," she said, with a smile more tentative than usual. She held out a small, folded piece of paper. "Uh, Mr. Weston asked us to give this to you." She said it apologetically.

Shayne Weston. The lover on whose boat Hannah had had her accident. Evan had met him for the first time—known of his existence for the first time—that night at the hospital.

Shayne had visited daily right after the accident, and made the drive every other week since they'd moved here several months later. He and Evan had worked out a visitation schedule that ensured they wouldn't cross paths again. Shayne had every other Sunday afternoon. Evan had every evening. Every evening for the last three-hundred and eighty-three days.

"Thank you, Ellie," he said quietly.

"You're welcome, sir." Evan wished she didn't feel like he needed such a sympathetic smile.

The door to Hannah's room slipped shut behind him with a *swish* like a broom. He was accustomed to the dimness of Hannah's room in the evening, but his eyes took a moment to adjust from the cheerless fluorescence of the hallway.

The only light in the room came from the machines that observed and reported her vital signs, and the small bedside lamp whose shade cast a slightly pink light around the room.

Evan stopped at her bed, as he always did, and rested his hands on the rail as he looked down at his wife. The beauty was still there, though her dark brown hair had lost its luster, and her normally tanned skin was pale and dull.

They'd only been married five years—no, now it was six. He hadn't actually grown used to having to be half of a whole when she'd fallen. Now he felt like a half with nothing to complete.

He walked around the foot of the bed, hiked up the knees of his pressed khakis, and sat in the little upholstered chair by the nightstand. He unfolded the piece of notepaper the nurse had handed him, read the handwritten paragraph quickly, then slipped the note into the small trash can by the bed.

"Dinkelman has been roused afresh by continuing vandalism," he said after a moment. "He hasn't even recovered from the shrubbery thing yet. I keep wanting to tell him we've arrested the Knights Who Say Nee, but the right moment just hasn't come yet. Of course, you and I both know it probably never will."

He shifted uneasily in his seat, re-crossing his legs instead of standing up to pace away a dim anger.

"Despite the man's attempts to appear British, he doesn't strike me as a Monty Python fan," he added.

He turned his head and looked out the window, though all he could see was the reflection of the room in which he was sitting.

"Shayne…" His voice cracked as he said the name. "Shayne's accepted a position in San Diego. He won't be able to visit anymore."

His jaw clenched, and he worked at relaxing it. Pity and regret helped dispel the anger, but slowly.

"I thought you should know, just in case he didn't tell you," he said quietly to the window. "It would be so sad for you to expect him."

# THREE

ON MONDAY, THE beauty of the April morning should have been enough to obliterate nearly any uneasiness of mind or spirit. The sky overhead was a cool, soft blue, not yet the sweltering white of summer. Tall cumulous clouds piled on the horizon, showing Florida their pretty side, while their dark underbellies hovered somewhere over the Gulf.

Evan figured he could work that into a metaphor, somehow, if he thought about it hard enough, but other things occupied his mind just now. Things from his past that Evan wished would stay in the past, things that robbed the splendid spring sky of its ability to calm the soul. Specifically, Sheriff Randall "Hutch" Hutchins, and the man who murdered him.

As he waited for a red light on Monumental, Evan lit a cigarette. Although Evan was otherwise what would be considered a health nut, he had picked up smoking somehow in college. He'd quit very shortly after he'd met Hannah. It had been tremendous work, and he'd allowed himself some pride, and relief, in his success.

He vividly remembered when he'd fallen again. It had been outside on the patio at the hospital, while Hannah was in surgery. When he recalled bumming the smoke from a man with an oxygen machine and a ratty blue robe, his memory always zoomed in on how his fingers had shaken when he'd reached for the cigarette. The next morning, he'd bought his first pack of Marlboros in six and a half years.

He had coddled himself, told himself that he would quit when this nightmare with Hannah was over; when she finally awoke. He snatched his thoughts away from his own life and thought about his former boss's.

The people Hutch had impacted in life would have considered him a good man. Even the few who hated him never would have pegged him for a wife beater. And worst of all, Hutch, himself, could not see himself as a wife beater. But rather than coming to terms with his inauthenticity and seeking help, the lovable hometown hero decided to end his own life. And even that wasn't the end of the troubles. Hutch had conspired to commit insurance fraud by disguising his suicide as a murder. He had conned a young man, Tommy Morrow, into pulling the trigger for him, in exchange for $8,500. He'd also convinced Tommy that it was the honorable thing to do.

Somehow, in a single stroke, by solving Hutch's murder, Evan had destroyed several lives, as well as the image Hutch had worked his whole life to construct. Within a week of Tommy's arrest, Hutch's widow had left her life-long home, without saying a word to her neighbors or friends. They all assumed she had gone to Pensacola to live with her daughter and son-in-law.

The money Hutch had given to Tommy now sat in the evidence locker, not financing anyone's college, or widowhood. Tommy's brother managed to make the football team for a second year, and thus keep his schol-arship, but some of the administrators were calling for an investigation into his involvement in Tommy's and Hutch's scheme. Evan didn't think the brother knew any-thing about what those two had cooked up. But, Tommy had been busted in the past for dealing pot and pawning stolen tools to finance his brother's school. Evan worried the school administrators wouldn't like what they saw if they delved too deeply into how Tommy's brother paid for everything the scholarship didn't cover.

Tommy, himself, had obtained the best public defend-er poverty could buy, a bedraggled but indefatigable, young lawyer with political ambitions named Abigail Abernathy. It was to an impromptu meeting with Ms. Abernathy ("call me Abby") that Evan now drove. She claimed to have new information that she felt Evan would like to know about before it "got out."

In his experience as a detective, defense attorneys always expected something in return for information offered. In his experience with Ms. Abernathy, Evan knew better than to have any expectations. His fascination with her legal creativity was offset by the tooth-grinding headaches her behind-the-scenes antics usually induced.

So far, Abby had filed motions to suppress, well, just about everything Evan's office produced, including the signed confession and all recordings of the interviews Evan and Wewahitchka Chief of Police, Nathan Beckett had conducted. She had filed a motion to have the case dismissed, claiming that if the State's allegations were true (which the defense does not concede) the entire case was built on an entrapment scheme and thus Tommy couldn't be charged anyway.

She filed a motion to the effect that Tommy did not have the mental acuity to understand that shooting Hutch in the back of the head with a .45 would kill him. She filed a motion stating that Tommy did not have the maturity to know right from wrong, especially in light of the fact that Hutch had been sort of a father figure to him, teaching him the few morals he managed to learn. Thus, when Hutch told him that shooting him in the back of the head was the right thing to do, Tommy had no basis on which to evaluate that statement, except that right and wrong boiled down to doing what "coach" said.

Evan knew none of these ploys could save Tommy. He was pretty sure Abby Abernathy knew it, too. She was losing money on the case, more than she'd make in a year as a public defender, he figured, and had no hope of helping Tommy in the least. She had a single purpose in taking the case, media exposure. The way she was flinging paper at the judge, this case might not go before a jury for months, maybe even a year, which meant it would have to show up on the nightly news at least two to three times a week for the foreseeable future. And every time it hit the news, the name Abby Abernathy would be repeated, seeding it deep in the minds of all her prospective constituents.

Then the trial would strike. The court clerk CC'd Evan on all documents regarding the Morrow case. He had traced the trajectory of the paper trail and had concluded that Abby was aiming to postpone the trial until October, just before the election. She had her eyes on a county council seat. It would be her first attempt at public office, and before Hutch turned up in a swamp with his mind all mixed up and spattered across the inside of his truck, it was a run she hadn't planned to win. She had wanted the name recognition and the experience so that two years later she could make a serious bid for a seat. But politicians are opportunists of the purest variety, and Abby knew that an opportunity like this might happen only once in a career, (though one could always hope for more).

What better dead horse to beat than a county council of old men who support a sheriff who abuses his wife and then hoodwinks some poor, low I.Q. kid into killing him to cover it up. It made a hell of a platform for her campaign. Add to that the year of free media attention she'd get from all her legal gymnastics, and the trial itself, which would be avidly followed by the vast majority of Gulf county residents, and Abby was looking like a front runner for the open seat.

Evan wished her God's speed. He hated the cut-throat, media-whore mentality of modern politicians, and saw no reason to think any better of Ms. Abernathy, but she was sticking up for Tommy Morrow. It might be the first time in Tommy's sad life that anyone was on his side, and for that, Evan determined to tolerate her.

He had left an hour early for shrimp and cheddar grits at the Sand Dollar Café, a popular Southern spot in Port St. Joe's quaintly hip downtown, hoping to grab a quick breakfast before his appointment with Ms. Abernathy, on the off chance that the meeting might mess with his appetite.

Vi Hartigan, his administrative assistant and self-appointed guardian, had been nagging him about his lost weight, again. Being able to show proof that he had eaten would make any interaction with her less stressful.

Pulling into an empty slot in front of the small café, Evan ground his cigarette into the ash tray and stepped out of his Pilot. He tilted his head back and inhaled through his nostrils, filling his lungs with the salt-tinged breeze. April was cooler here than it was back in Cocoa Beach or Miami. The air seemed cleaner, too, with a better chance of providing some kind of refreshment.

He released the breath, slowly, centering himself, and intentionally putting all thoughts of Tommy, Abby and Hutch out of his mind. Also, Hannah, he would not think of her, either. Or the boyfriend who was leaving her. For the next half-hour, he would eat his shrimp and cheddar grits and enjoy it like a normal person with a normal life.

Sun glinted off the glass and chrome of the parked vehicles as he moved around them to the entrance. A balmy slip of breeze twitched at his lapel on one side and cooled his cheek. He allowed the corner of his mouth to lift in the hint of a smile as he reached for the door. His reflection stared back at him in the glass. As he swung it open, the content reflection of his own face was replaced by County Councilman James Quillen's angry scowl. When Quillen's eyes met Evan's, his scowl hardened.

The councilman swung his head around to glare at someone standing behind him, Ms. Abernathy of all people. Beside Ms. Abernathy, an incredibly uncomfortable looking hostess did her best to hide behind a fan of menus. Abby stood with her hands clasped in front of her waist, eyes big and bright as new-minted nickels, and a smile on her delicate lips that looked sweet enough to make Goff's coffee palatable. Her silky blond hair coiled atop her head in a structure that could feel equally at home in a New York law firm or an Amy Brown painting. Two corkscrewed tresses dangled strategically at the edge of her left eye. She wore a conservative skirt suit, light in both weight and color, but her demeanor suggested she would be more comfortable in something with polka dots.

When Quillen turned back to Evan, his face was at least two shades redder. He looked back at Abby one more time, wheeled on Evan, and growled, "This has got to stop! You call me as soon as you are done with her." Then he pushed passed Evan and stormed into the formerly beautiful day.

Evan looked to Ms. Abernathy, and he could tell he was still smiling. In fact, he had to fight the impulse to laugh out loud at how such a dainty flower could so effortlessly fillet the head of the Gulf County Commissioners. Perhaps there was hope for Tommy yet.

Of course, Evan would be on the chopping block next. That thought brought his smile under control quickly.

She blinked at him, and cocked her head, just slightly, "You're early."

"I am," Evan agreed. "I'm also hungry. I'm planning on having some breakfast before…"

"Oh, don't be silly," she said, cranking up the wattage on her smile. The light in her eyes was real, Evan was sure of that, but the smile he trusted not one bit. "This will only take a minute. Let's grab a table!" She said it like an invitation to embark on some grand adventure.

Escaping his boat without claw marks in his slacks or pee in his shoe had been enough adventure for Evan today. He stepped through the entryway, nodding to the hostess, (her tentative smile had been bolstered by Abby's sanguinity,) and let the door fall closed behind him. The crisp spring breeze was gone, swallowed by the dim and overly air-conditioned interior of The Sand Dollar.

"Besides," Abby said, "we're both on the county dime."

Her voice had a tendency, he'd noticed, to tilt upwards at the ends of her sentences, like she was asking a question. He found it simultaneously annoying and disarming.

"Ms. Abernathy…" he began, intending to tell her that he meant to have his breakfast first, and to explain that he was salaried, so the notion of whose dime he was on wasn't particularly relevant. Then his phone rang.

Abby's smile shifted a bit, in a parody of despair, and she rolled her eyes as if to say, of course.

"I'll get us a table while you…" She gestured at his phone. "Want some coffee?"

"It's Dinkelman," Evan said, flatly, looking at the phone's display.

"Nice!" Abby whispered, moving toward the hostess. She wiggled one craftily sculpted eyebrow, and gave Evan a thumbs-up. Either she was too excited about whatever it was that lit her fire to notice Evan's look of distain, or she intentionally ignored it. Apparently, a call from Dinkelman meant something entirely different to her than it did to him.

Evan let himself back outside and hit the answer button on his phone. "Caldwell," he said.

"They destroyed the evidence!" Dinkelman growled into his ear. "I told you this would happen."

"Who destroyed what evidence?" Evan asked.

"If I knew who did it, I wouldn't be calling you!" Dinkelman said. "Your yellow tape didn't do a damn thing."

"George, what do you mean they 'destroyed' the evidence?"

"Oh! Oh, ho ho, you're gonna love this, Mister most-folks-are-respectful! These vandals found themselves a bowling ball somewhere, and they used the beer bottles as pins! There's broken glass everywhere!"

This last bit he shouted into his phone, causing Evan to wince and draw back.

"I told you, you should have sent someone out last night," Dinkelman continued. "Maybe next time you'll listen to me. Who are you going to send to clean up this mess?"

"I thought I told you to put them in your office."

"I thought it best not to disturb the evidence."

"Well, as long as *you* thought it best," Evan replied. He sighed. "Has the scene tech been there yet?"

"What? That elf-eared woman?" Dinkelman asked. "She's even less helpful than you are. She suggested I get a dog!"

The comment about Paula's ear pissed him off just a little, but the rest of Dinkelman's complaint made Evan smile. He knew she'd have heard it as a compliment.

"And she collected the evidence?" Evan asked.

"What was left of it," Dinkelman scoffed. "She got the ball. And a few of the larger pieces of glass."

"Okay," Evan said, then paused before adding, "so, what is the purpose of this call?" He almost asked if Dinkelman wanted more police tape, but restrained himself.

There was a flustered blustering on the other end, but Evan could not decipher any actual words. He told himself that he absolutely was not hoping Dinkelman was stroking out.

"Mr. Dinkelman," Evan tried again.

"'What is the purpose…' The purpose? The purpose is…is to report that a crime has been committed! And the perpetrator has destroyed the evidence because you did not, did not, do your job! The purpose is to let you know that there are criminals. Running wild. In your town. That, Sheriff, is the purpose. There are criminals. And I am reporting them!"

The line went dead. Evan assumed George had hung up on him. It was undoubtedly the nicest thing Dinkelman had done all day.

# FOUR

ABBY SAT IN a small corner booth with an open laptop to her right, an open leather brief case to her left, and a huge omelet directly in front of her. Across from her, at the booth's only other place setting, sat a bowl of shrimp and slowly hardening grits. He wondered if he'd mentioned his intended order to her, or she'd just remembered it from the first time he'd been cajoled into having breakfast with her. Maybe she was keeping a database of factoids to use against him in court someday.

"Oh, there you are!" Abby said, looking up from her screen. "How did it go with George?" she asked, and her tone made Evan wonder if, somewhere in her head, it was Christmas morning and she was still six. "He sure is an odd fellow, isn't he?" She took a feminine bite of her gargantuan veggie omelet. "But I like him. Eccentric, right? That's the word, for a guy like that?"

"That's one word you could use," Evan allowed.

Abby's lips pouted, but her eyes twinkled, "Aw, come on now. He just sees things a little differently. Nothing wrong with that, is there? Oh, I should tell you," Abby said, reaching across and patting the top of his hand lightly. "We're having dinner tonight, George and I. Sounds like he's got a lot on his mind."

Evan smiled evenly. "I guess I should be happy about that," he said. "Let him into your life and you'll have no time left to bother me."

She pursed her lips and studied Evan for a moment, seeming to decide to which part of his comment she would respond. Then her face brightened. "Oh, I know how to handle guys like him," she laughed dismissively. "But I think he deserves to be heard. Look at how many jobs he's brought to our town."

"'Our town' is going to need a few more officers on the police force to keep up with him once the annexation goes through," Evan countered.

"If it goes through," Abby said. "A bunch of those families who've lived in the county their whole lives kinda like things the way they are. There's more opposition than the county council lets on. But more cops means more local employment, right?"

Evan noticed the speed with which her girlishness disappeared when matters of business snuck into the conversation. He wondered which persona was real and which was the mask.

"I don't imagine you asked to see me about the annexation, Ms. Abernathy—"

"Oh, call me Abby," she said. "Looks like we're going to be seeing a lot of each other in the coming months. Might as well be friendly about it."

Again, Evan felt a slight disagreement with her choice of adjectives when describing their relationship, but this time he kept it to himself. He gave her a quick, polite smile, then nodded and returned to the topic at hand. "What would you like to talk about this morning, Abby?"

"Okay," she said, and Evan could not tell if the faint edge in her voice indicated that his abruptness had truly offended, or if it was just more of her façade. "Straight to business, then," she continued. "Sheriff Caldwell, I need to know, do you consider yourself an honest man?"

Evan had enough experience around defense attorneys to not be surprised by much. The question did not catch him off guard. "Why do you ask?"

She laughed, "I guess we need to define 'honest.' Answering a question with a question is evasion, not quite lying, but not exactly truthful either. So, is that honest? Or dishonest?" Before Evan could speak, she quickly held up both hands and said, "No… don't answer that, we'll both be trading questions all day."

Her light laughter nearly drew the same response from Evan, but he managed to contain it.

"Here's what I see," Abby continued. "You view me as an opponent, which is, you know, to be expected. You being with the prosecution and me with the defense and all. But, I am also one of your constituents, right? And as such, I need to know if I can trust you. Do you mean what you say? I have the right to expect an answer to a question like that, don't I?" She didn't quite bat her eyelashes, but the rest of her facial expression would have supported such a gesture.

Evan felt a warning sent from the hairs on his forearms. "I suppose you do," he said. "So, yes, I do consider myself to be an honest man."

"Huh." She looked confused. "I would have thought so, too. I'm a bit bewildered, though. You see, you told me you arrived early because you were hungry and wanted to eat. But, we've been here almost ten minutes already and you haven't even touched your food."

Evan said nothing. Her confusion was pretense and her attempted point annoyed him. He studied her face. There was glee beneath her puzzled expression and Evan found it fascinating to watch her try to conceal it. What he didn't know was whether the glee was innocent fun or more the sadistic kind.

"I mean, I know you love shrimp and grits," she went on. "And rumor has it, you'll travel several blocks out of your way for *cafe con leche*. So, I know the problem isn't with the food."

Evan leaned back and folded his arms. "Ms. Abernathy." She opened her mouth to interrupt but he stopped her with his hand and continued. "We are not meeting as friends, we are not meeting for breakfast, and if you wish to discuss civics or politics, you can do so through our Public Information Officer."

"You know, Sheriff Caldwell, I'm pretty good at getting what I want. I think it's kind of fun that you're not easily ruffled or pushed over."

She dabbed at lips that didn't need dabbing, gracefully stabbed a petite morsel of tomato with her fork, considered it a moment, and raised it to her mouth. The bite was small enough that it didn't hinder her from finishing her thought. "I really do like you, you know. I get that you're not a politician at heart, so, you're kind of like a non-combatant in these upcoming elections. But you're also right in the middle of things, which means, if there is any...what do they call it?" She paused, then leaned forward and asked, "What's that word for when there's a battle and a bunch of civilians get wiped out?"

"Collateral damage?" Evan offered. He was growing weary of the simple girl act. She'd managed to make it through law school.

"Yes," she exclaimed, eyes twinkling, "Collateral damage! You're right in the middle of this thing. So, if there is any collateral damage, I'm afraid you're probably going to be it. And, as your friend, constituent, and admirer, I would hate to see that happen."

Evan set his cup down and waited a moment to see if she had more to offer. When she didn't he said, "Well, to be honest, I'm not looking forward to it either."

She didn't reply right away. He could tell she was less excited about his non-responsiveness than she had claimed to be. The coffee had been delicious, and now that the taste was on his palate, he wanted more. He decided to go ahead and eat. He really was hungry, and sitting here listening to Abigail Abernathy trying to tangle him up in words had gotten boring pretty quickly.

Turning his attention to the food, and thereby casually dismissing her, solved both problems. The shrimp and grits were just as good as the coffee, though cooler than he generally liked them. His empty stomach fired off signals of gratitude to his brain with the first swallow – and Ms. Abernathy finally started approaching the matter she had clearly been circling all morning.

"We need to talk about the Morrow case," she said.

Evan nodded. "How is he holding up?"

"He'd be doing a lot better if Chimes wasn't trying to ride him to re-election."

"District Attorney Chimes?" Evan asked. "You think he's going to go hard on Tommy for the press?"

"Well, of course!"

"I'd think he'd want to avoid a trial. He was close with Hutchins," Evan said. Abby was shaking her head, but he continued. "Seems like you could use that to Tommy's advantage. This is an ugly case and anyone associated with it is gonna get tainted. I would think Chimes would love to offer Tommy a plea to keep it out of the courtroom next year. And the papers."

"Oh, you'd like that, wouldn't you?" she asked teasingly. "If we just roll over and wet on ourselves? No. Tommy's gonna walk. You'll see."

Evan stared at her for a moment. "You can't possibly believe that."

"I'm the Gloria Allred of Gulf County," she said, "and I've got better hair."

Evan continued to favor her with his flat stare. "Allred's a discrimination attorney."

"Minor difference," she said stonily. "Look, what happened to Tommy was wrong. And now Chimes wants to give him the chair so he'll have something to boast about come November. Are you going to tell me that's *justice*?"

"No. You're right. Hutch used him, and now, from what you're saying, it sounds like Chimes is planning on using him, too."

"See, we found some common ground," she said, brightly. She leaned forward and patted his hand. Her nose scrunched a little as she said, "Maybe we can be friends after all."

That worried Evan, so he decided to move the conversation away from their looming friendship. "Have you been to see Tommy recently? How's he doing?"

"Well, he's done some time in the past," she said, "quite a bit I guess. So, that's not as hard on him as it would normally be on a kid of his age and mental capacity. The Sheriff's Office really did a number on him, though. I think that trauma will be with the poor kid for the rest of his life."

Evan found his smile easily this time, but not his nice smile. "So, you are planning to sue the county in civil court on Tommy's behalf," he said, shaking his head. "I guess you've got a better chance with that than with his criminal case. Murdering a friend, a father figure no less, in cold blood, for a little bit of money. Knowing Tommy, I'm sure that it was horribly traumatic, but the jury isn't going to let him walk just because he was manipulated into killing Hutch. Hutchins was a hometown hero for decades."

Abby's face hardened. "Are you really taking Hutch's side?" she demanded, "after all he's done? Maybe I should just let you take the fall for all this." She placed her flat hand on a thick envelope that lay amid the clutter of paperwork surrounding her.

It was all part of her setup. The folder had been there since before he had sat down. She could have referred to it at any time, but she had waited until the mood and timing suited her purposes. He put his fork down beside the plate and sat back in his chair. The shrimp and grits no longer interested him.

"As you will recall," Evan said in a deliberately calm tone, "I was the one who discovered Hutch's issues, and I did nothing to conceal any of it. I don't take sides here, Ms. Abernathy, that's your job. Now, if you have something there in that folder that you'd like to show me, well, I guess I'll take a look. Otherwise, I need to get back to *my* job."

She heaved a great sigh and drew the folder front and center, but still did not open it. She stared at Evan for a moment, trying to get a read on him. Then sighed again and said, "You know how this goes. A case like this. You've got that poor kid stitched up six ways from Sunday and somehow, I have to try to help him. Call it taking sides if you like, but that *is* my job. The people of this county pay me to do it and I take that responsibility very seriously. It is my job and I am going to give it everything I've got." She shrugged. "It's the only way I know."

Evan watched her. He felt sure he was seeing a slightly truer version of herself than she normally revealed.

She continued. "The only way I can see to help Tommy at trial is to discredit the prosecution. And, like it or not, that includes you." She patted the file. "It also includes a handful of other characters. Your pal, Chief Beckett, is high on that list. I know the two of you worked together to get a," she lifted her fingers in air-quotes, "'confession' out of Tommy. Without any legal representation present, I might add."

Evan folded his arms and waited for her.

She glared at him for a second, continuing to pat the envelope lightly. "I've already got plenty to work with on that guy, and I'd like to keep my focus on him, rather than dragging you down, too, if I can manage it. I think it's in everybody's best interest, the best interest of the Gulf County residents, who you and I both represent, to work toward reestablishing their faith in the Sheriff's Office." She nodded at him. "Don't you think?"

"You want me to help you take down Beckett? You really think that's going to do anything to help your client?" Evan scoffed. "And you honestly expect me to believe you could hang this on a small-town police chief without tainting the Sheriff's Office as well?" He shook his head and let a wry grin move across his lips. "You are clever, Ms. Abernathy, but I doubt the devil himself is that clever."

"If I don't have enough on Beckett to get that confession thrown out, I will have to come after you," she said, sliding the folder across the table to him, but not lifting her hand from it. "Evan, I don't want to do that. I think you're a good man. I think you're just the kind of man this county needs as sheriff. But, I have a responsibility to my client. I know he isn't innocent, but I also know that he was set up, and sending him to the electric chair is just wrong. Help me out here. Don't make me use this stuff."

She finally released the file and sat back, folding her hands demurely in her lap. The facial expression she had decided on for this part of the meeting said, please don't be mad. Evan wasn't buying it, but he wanted to.

He took the folder and opened it. Dividers separated the contents into five separate files, each with a tab describing its contents. Two were labeled Police Brutality. The third read Illegal Search and Seizure. The fourth,

Cruelty to Animals. The last tab proclaimed Inappropriate Contact with a Minor.

Evan looked up from the document and met Abby's eyes. He made no attempt to hide his disapproval. She held his gaze for just a moment, then looked down at her coffee. Steam no longer rose from it.

Evan turned back to the files. He opened the first Police Brutality file and was met with the grimacing meth-pecked mug of Ricky Nickels. Had the situation been different in any way, Evan probably would not have been able to choke back a laugh, or at least a snort. He didn't bother to read the report behind the photo. He flicked his eyes up to Abby again, his not-nice smile sneaking onto his face.

"I don't have to convict you, Evan." Her truth showed in her eyes, and on the blush rising in her cheeks. But the embarrassment was tempered by a defiance bordering on petulance, "just have to discredit you…and your men."

Evan felt his own cheeks color just a bit. He knew she was right. His anger was not directed primarily at her, but at a system that had slipped so far out of sync with itself that it now incentivized attacking the very ones who protected it.

He flipped open the next folder and was not surprised to see a glossy 8X10 of Mac McMillian. It was probably a studio publicity photo he had made up to apply for modeling jobs. Evan guessed the shot had been taken before the musclebound moron had bounced his pretty face off the deck of his own boat in a failed attempt at eluding police.

This, too, was funny, but it was also more problematic than the Nickels file. If Ms. Abernathy really felt she could push the envelope that far, she could use this photo, compare it to the slightly altered angle of Mac-Mac's post-arrest nose, and claim that Evan's "excessive" force was not only brutal, but had also ended poor Mac-Mac's dreams of becoming a famous underwear model, or action movie star.

"You know, this guy's parents are pretty well off." Evan said. "The kid has the whole entitled-trust-fund-baby thing down to a science. Maybe give his dad a call. I'm sure the old man would kick in a few thousand to Morrow's defense fund if you tell him you're going after me."

"Tried that," she said, glumly, then offered a wan smile in response to Evan's raised eyebrows.

She shook her head. "Mac is estranged from his parents. He's supposed to be at university in England right now. Instead, he invested his tuition money in that charter business of his. Only thing the dad's upset at you for is 'cause you only broke one of his wrists."

"You have been busy," Evan said. "What else have you tried?"

This time, she did bat her lashes, "Turn the page."

Under the tab marked *Illegal Search and Seizure* was a series of depositions that had been taken from employees of the Port St. Joe Department of Licensure, their version of the DMV. Evan scanned the documents, noting that the depositions had been taken by someone other than Abby, and that they were all dated just two days ago. The questions were steeply slanted, cornering the unsuspecting Department of Licensure clerks into crooked answers.

The picture painted by the depositions, when taken together, suggested that Evan had strong-armed Goff's cousin Audrey into providing him with information he had no legal right to see. The accusation was, of course, spurious. But the documents also conveyed a veiled threat – if Evan didn't play ball, Abernathy could take these depositions to the Florida State DOL headquarters and possibly seek disciplinary action against Goff's cousin, maybe even get her fired.

This was when Evan decided that Abby was a snake. For all her cute enthusiasm and girlish exuberance, she was deceitful and poisonous. And she could shed her skin to take on whatever face the moment required. Breakfast was over.

He closed the folder and started to slide it back across the table.

"But wait," she said, trying for a fun parody of a late-night TV junk huckster. "There's more."

The joke was too true to be funny. Evan gave her a hard stare before looking back down at the folder. The next tab read *Cruelty to Animals*. When he flipped it open, he saw several stills taken from the security cameras at Pet Warehouse depicting Evan evaluating cat harnesses, and eventually purchasing one. These were followed by black-and-white photos of him and Plutes on his boat, Plutes wrapped up in harnesses and bungees. These latter had been taken by a professional grade camera through a telephoto lens. The harness had been an experiment he'd tried a couple of times, and it had failed to be a safer or more agreeable set-up for either Evan or the damn cat. He'd gone back to the backpack. Now the cat was happy and Evan had neck issues, but the photos painted a different picture.

The deposition from the twelve-year-old-looking kid from Pet Warehouse who had sold him the harness stated that said kid believed the sheriff intended to use the cat as bait for bull sharks. This was followed by notes regarding other PSJ residents and visitors who recalled seeing Evan on his boat trying to stuff a "stray cat" into what, "might have been a burlap sack".

Evan looked across the table, his green eyes cold with anger. "That's my cat and he happens to like riding on the boat," he said, his voice sharp as a Bowie knife. "I was trying to figure out a way to keep him from going overboard."

"Out of twelve jurors," Abby asked in her no nonsense, attorney voice, "How many are really going to believe that your cat actually wanted to be in that harness?"

"He didn't," Evan said. "That's why we went back to the backpack. It's like surfing for him."

"I've had cats my whole life," she said, and he was too angry to think that figured. "As a species, they seldom surf."

Evan invisibly let out a calming breath. "Well, I've *never* had a cat, and as a species, I find them pretty damn baffling." He looked back down at the paperwork without seeing it.

"I think it would be interesting to hear you try to explain that your cat surfs." She paused, then added, "Especially after you tell them where the cat came from?"

Evan tried to give himself a moment by staring at the folder. He felt a chill pass through his chest and up his neck. Not the chill of fear, but of rage.

"I mean, your wife's lover gave her that cat, right?" she said.

When he thought he might be able to speak without yelling, he looked back up at Abernathy.

"Who told you that?" he asked, his tone chilly.

"It doesn't matter." She must have seen the rage in his eyes. It didn't seem to bother her. She shrugged at him in a parody of apology. "Aw, you just realized I'm the kind of person who plays to win."

"Actually, I just realized that you lack the common decency to be considered any kind of person at all," he said quietly.

He saw something shift in her eyes, so fleeting that it was gone before he could define it.

"Well," she said, shaking her hair just a bit. "Then you'll probably really disapprove of that last bit there."

Evan looked back down at the folder reluctantly, steeling himself, but not nearly enough.

The final tab read *Inappropriate Contact with a Minor*. The only minor Evan had any contact with these days was Sarah, and he'd never even been alone with her in private. If Abernathy intended to drag her into this, he would have to take Abby more seriously, and he would have to be very careful not to let her bait him into some kind of rage-fueled response. Evan had never raised a hand to a woman and he never would, but at this moment he could have shot her.

He opened this final tab. It contained several photos, apparently taken with the same telephoto camera as the Plutes photos. Evan was struck by the amount of money and time Abby had committed to just his part of her case.

The first photo showed Evan helping Sarah onto his boat. He held two glass bottles in the hand not holding hers. He remembered the day. Sarah had brought the bottles of fizzy fruit drinks, called Izzies, over for Evan to try, and they'd had them out on the deck, in full view of anyone and everyone. But viewing the black-and-white photo, a casual observer would assume the bottles contained beer.

The next photo was equally disingenuous. Evan and Sarah trying to wrestle Plutes out of his surfing harness before the damn cat had even given it a chance. That's how Evan remembered it, but the angle of the camera did not capture Plutes at all. Instead, it kinda looked like Evan and Sarah were dancing, very close.

The file held two more photos that could be seen one way or another, that might have seemed suggestive of inappropriate behavior, depending on how badly someone wanted to see it that way.

"We didn't actually come up with much on that one," she said, almost apologetically. "I guess if we had, I wouldn't be having breakfast with you right now."

"You didn't really come up with much on any of them, did you?" Evan asked, his voice smooth but cold. "And you are not having breakfast with me. You are attempting to blackmail me with garbage, and you are attempting to wreak havoc on innocent people's lives."

Evan pinned her with his stare, and he saw her shoulder twitch just a bit, like the coldness in his eyes was drifting across the distance to chill her skin.

She held his gaze with an effort, but she lost most of the pretense of dominance she had affected throughout their meeting. All that was left in her face now was defiance and that childish stubbornness. It was not lost on Evan, though, that stubbornness of that intensity had been known to topple much greater opposition than he had to offer. And there was nothing childish about it. It lacked that innocence.

When she said nothing, he continued. "These accusations are not just stupid, they're dangerous. They will hurt people, good people. Do you understand that?"

She was still silent, her jaw clamped down so tightly Evan feared her back teeth might crack.

"It's unethical and dangerous to fling these accusations around just to advance your own personal agenda,"

Evan pushed. "We both know the only reason you took this case is to win a seat on the County Council."

The color in her cheeks became more natural. Her eyes lit up, true fire this time, no pretense at all. She kept her voice low, so as not to make a scene, but Evan heard fury in her words. "And we both know this county needs better representation. What happened to Tommy was wrong. What happened to Marlene was wrong. And all of it went on right under the watchful eye of those old men. So, yeah, I want on that council. I want to bust some skulls up there. But it's not my, 'own personal agenda.'" She repeated his phrase back at him with a depth of sardonic vitriol that was almost convincing in its self-righteousness. "It's because this county deserves better than the likes of James Quillen and his cronies."

Evan felt her anger infecting him, and conflicting him. He didn't disagree with her opinion, and he wouldn't have found fault with her for her passion, if she'd kept it above-board, ethical, and true. But she'd crossed a line that didn't get uncrossed.

He waited to see if her speech had concluded. When it seemed it had, he drew a deep breath and said, "You are well aware that this," he tapped the folder, "is an empty jacket. There is nothing here. You are also aware that this is a witch hunt with a dangerously broad net, and decent people will be drowned in it if you spread it as rumors in an attempt to taint the jury pool. You do either, and I will see to it that you are disbarred, Ms. Abernathy. If it's at all possible, I will also have you arrested. I'll have to consult an honorable attorney to see how I can best manage that."

He stood and dropped a twenty on the half-eaten breakfast Abby had intended to buy for him.

She stood as well, seeming not the least bit chastened by his warning or ashamed of her tactics. "I am just trying to right a wrong, Sheriff." She delivered the line as if she were the widow heroine in some 1960's western movie.

"How many wrongs are you planning to commit in the process?" he asked.

She didn't immediately reply, but Evan figured if he stuck around a second too long, she would. He didn't think he could maintain any civility at that point.

"I hope you got some satisfaction from your shots fired," he said, and he saw a bit of a smile at the corner of her mouth. "Enough to sustain you when you reap the results. Your aim was exceptionally unfortunate."

He got just a glimpse of her disappearing smile before he turned and stalked away.

# FIVE

WHEN EVAN ENTERED the reception area in front of his office, Vi Hartigan was standing behind her desk, her chin tilted toward the ceiling as she peered down through her bifocals at her computer screen. Their bead-encrusted chain rattled as she looked up at Evan.

Vi was in her mid-sixties, a slim woman with down-like red hair that she kept cut short. Her hawkish nose and thin, unsmiling lips kept her from being pretty, but she still managed to strike Evan as some form of hand-some. Wearing knee-length white Bermuda shorts and a turquoise polo shirt that matched her woven belt, Vi looked as though she should be joining friends on their boat. In the eighties.

"Mr. Caldwell," she intoned in her Barbara Stanwy-ck timbre. She never called him Sheriff or even Evan. "Good morning."

She reached into an inbox surrounded by little aloe plants, pictures of her four cats, and a tea mug with a little ceramic lid, and removed a handful of pink message slips. She considered voice mail a tool of the dark world, or at the very least a personal affront to her capabilities.

"Good morning, Vi," Evan said as he stopped beside her desk. English breakfast tea and Shalimar wafted gently in the air around her.

Vi removed her glasses and let them fall against her chest. "Deputy Hammond's mother is still in the ICU so he remains on family leave. I've removed him from the roster for the whole of the week, just in case. McCoy volunteered for overtime, should that be necessary. He's nigh upon having the money for an above-ground pool. Hilton offered you one free night at their new property in Destin. I've accepted it in your stead. Also," she added with a sigh, "Mr. Dinkelman conveyed intense upset at continued vandalism. He's disgusted with your inability to apprehend those responsible. He also suggested that you look into local landscapers and developers who might be pilfering his vegetation to save some money."

She held the stack of pink message slips out for him. He raised his eyebrows at her and she frowned as she tilted them into her trash can.

"I suspect that Dinkelman actually enjoys intense upset," Evan said. He tapped Abby Abernathy's file against the leg of his navy-blue suit pants. "So, I met with Abby Abernathy this morning."

"She'll never be taken seriously until she gets married."

"I'm taking her pretty seriously at the moment," Evan replied. At Vi's intensified frown, he held up the offensive folder. "It appears her first line of defense for Tommy Morrow is going to be to discredit us, me in particular. She's got someone running around digging up dirt."

"This is unconscionable behavior," Vi said, shaking her head. Her big gold hoops jangled in percussive agreement. "What sort of dirt can she possibly be after?"

"I'll fill you in on it later," Evan answered. "I just want you to be on the alert."

"I'm always on the alert," Vi said with a hint of indignation.

"My mistake," Evan said. "Goff in yet?"

"Sgt. Goff is in the break room, feeding his pet mustache," she answered.

"Do me a favor and ask him to come back here, okay?"

Vi turned toward her desk phone, and Evan opened the door to his office. He left it open behind him as he walked to his desk, took off his blazer, and draped it neatly over the back of his chair. Then he sat down in the leather office chair that he couldn't seem to grow to like but wasn't willing to replace, either.

He had just opened Abby Abernathy's problematic folder when the intercom buzzed.

"Yes, Vi," he answered.

"This is Vi," she said. "Sgt. Goff is on his way and Hank Paulsen with the Lions Club is on line two. He's hoping you've decided on something to donate for the fundraiser next week."

Evan sighed. "I was kind of hoping I'd have some crime scene evidence or something, you know, something exciting, but it's been a slow week."

Vi was silent for just a moment. Then, "I'm due to take my break in twelve minutes," she said. "Perhaps we could trade witticisms then."

Evan tried not to smile. "If you can work it in."

"What would you like me to tell Hank Paulsen?" she asked.

"Do you have any suggestions?"

"We have a few extra softball jackets," she answered.

"Sounds good to me."

A few minutes later, Evan heard Sgt. Ruben Goff and Vi exchange perfunctory greetings, and Goff ambled into Evan's office. At five-eight and no more than one hundred and twenty pounds, Goff was a wire hanger of a man whose hips barely supported his gun belt. The heftiest part of Goff was his salt and pepper mustache, which he kept trimmed only to a suggestion of compliance with the facial hair regulations. Goff's appearance suggested he was the love child of Sam Elliot and Don Knotts, but he was smart as hell, cooler than a cucumber in the midst of chaos, and a miraculously accurate sharpshooter.

"Hey, boss," Goff said as he came in. He was carrying a small pink Tupperware container in one hand and a fork in the other.

"Hey, Goff. Sit down a minute, huh?" Evan said.

Goff deposited himself in one of the two orange vinyl chairs in front of Evan's desk and held the Tupperware up. "'Scuse me for eating in front of you, but the beautiful one sent me off with pie this morning, and it won't do to leave it unattended in the break room."

Goff's wife could have passed for his twin, except for her unruly red hair. If Goff hadn't been the first one to accept Evan as acting sheriff, Evan would have liked him for his devotion to his wife of forty-some years.

"Don't worry about it," Evan replied. "Actually, you might want to finish it before I ruin your appetite."

"Well, that sounds promising," the other man said. He took his last bite of what looked to be blueberry pie, then put the fork inside the Tupperware and set it on his lap. He looked up at Evan expectantly.

"I had a little get-together with Abby Abernathy, Tommy Morrow's lawyer," Evan said.

"That's about as calamitous a name as I've ever heard, but I hope she gets that kid a break," Goff said.

"Well, she's certainly trying," Evan replied. "Unfortunately, she's trying to do it by proving us incompetent, unethical, or worse."

"Hell, you say."

Evan tapped his fingers against the open file folder. "I'm pretty sure she's hired somebody to discredit us—

and, in particular, me—whether by means of illegal search and seizure, violation of the Privacy Act, or what have you. I'm going to let you read the file, but I don't want anyone else to know what's in here yet."

"What are you telling me for?" Goff asked, but his squinty frown indicated he had some idea why.

"Because she knows your cousin gave us information on a state employee without a search warrant."

"Hell's bells, we were after a serial killer!" Goff exclaimed. "Reckon she wouldn't have minded it so much if she'd been the next one on the list."

"But she wasn't, so she does," Evan said. "Even if she thought we were justified, she'd still use it. She wants to make a name for herself with this case."

"Well, she sure as hell could use a new one," Goff said. "How'd she find out Audrey helped us?"

"I don't know," Evan answered. "But it just became my first priority to find out. In the meantime, you might want to give your cousin a heads-up. And I need you to take point on the Dinkelman thing."

"You're not doin' much for my positive outlook this morning," Goff said, his mustache twitching.

"My apologies. But he apparently had some trespassers out there last night, and he's all up in his stumpy arms about it," Evan said. "I sent Trigg out there to see if she could get some prints off some empty beer bottles, but apparently, the bad guys were back last night and broke all of the evidence. I don't know if she got any prints or not; she's not back yet."

Goff sighed. "People stealing stuff to sell don't usually hang around vandalizing the scene, at least, not in my experience."

"Just see what Paula came up with, and then let's appease this guy by taking a look at some of the local landscapers, see if something politely jumps out at us."

"I thought we were thinking somebody was stealin' them for drugs," Goff said.

"And they might be, but who are they selling shrubs *to*?"

"Gotcha."

Evan sighed and sat back in his chair. "If it wasn't such a slow week, I'd have Crenshaw or somebody do it, but I don't really need you on anything else at the moment. Besides, you're a lot more patient than I am."

"Remember you said that when I end up slappin' some sense into him," Goff said. "That man's half a bubble shy of plumb if you ask me."

"No argument from me," Evan muttered. "Just see if you can keep him placated until we can excuse ourselves to work a nice murder case or something."

"Been slow this month," Goff said, rubbing the corners of his mustache down. "I even wrote a ticket this morning."

"I appreciate that."

Evan spent the rest of his slow Monday catching up on paperwork, appearing in court, which was just across the parking lot, for a five-minute bail hearing, and trying to track down Nathan Beckett, his erstwhile counterpart with Wewahitchka PD. Beckett didn't seem to want to answer his cell or return his voice mail messages, but Evan liked the guy enough to want to warn him about Abby Abernathy. Unwilling to state his business over voice mail, he left one last message for Beckett to call him back, marked it urgent, then hung up and left for the day.

Evan made a quick stop at the Piggly Wiggly near the marina entrance, to pick up some pork chops and a gallon of milk. The day had developed a bit of wind to it as it went on, and the air had the definite tang of brine as Evan made his way down the pier.

His boat was at the T-head, and the two slips before it were empty at the moment, so Evan was taken aback when he heard the faint sound of music coming from near the end of the dock. He slowed his steps for a moment, then picked up his pace as he determined that the music was definitely coming from his boat.

He unlocked the French door from the sundeck and jerked it open.

Plutes was perched on the arm of the couch like Poe's raven, facing the door. On the floor in front of the end table, still plugged into the charger, Evan's iPad was lying facedown.

James Taylor was singing about how Evan's smiling face made him smile, which Evan found peculiar, since James Taylor wasn't on any of his playlists. He stared at Plutes.

"Does Apple know you can do that?" he asked.

The cat gave him one slow blink of disdain and then looked away.

# SIX

TUESDAY MORNING, EVAN made it from the parking lot to the front door of the Sheriff's office before Dinkelman was summoning him on his cell phone. Evan was hellbent on drinking the *café con leche* in his travel mug before being required to interact with anyone, least of all Dinkelman.

He considered letting it ring through to voice mail, then trying to get his coffee in before Dinkelman tried again, but in the end, he decided his best bet would be to answer the phone now, tell Dinkelman he now had his own deputy, and pawn him off on Goff as quickly as possible.

It was a good plan, and like most good plans, it fell apart as soon as it was implemented.

When he accepted the call, no voice greeted him at the other end. At least, it didn't sound like a voice. If anything, it sounded like Plutes clearing a massive hairball.

"Mr. Dinkelman?" Evan tried. "George?"

The wheezing, hacking spluttering continued, still not accompanied by any words, though a few discernable squeaks had worked their way into his monologue.

Evan noticed Goff ambling across the back parking lot towards his cruiser, tin lunch pail in hand, the same lunch pail Goff's wife had been devotedly packing for probably just about as long as Evan had been alive. Goff's impossibly narrow shadow spilled out ahead of him in the bright spring morning. For a moment Evan wondered how such a creature came to be, and how he had found himself liking so much a man who could not be more different from Evan.

The feeble but frenetic attempt at communication across the phone lines drew his attention back to the present. George Dinkelman had managed a word or two, but the words didn't go together to form a thought. Evan wondered if the man might actually be having a heart attack or stroke.

He waved at Goff to hurry, and the diminutive man's spiny little legs worked double-time, his gun belt squeaking and creaking in harmony.

As Goff approached the wide concrete steps, Dinkelman finally squeezed out an actual word. "Body!" was the word in question.

"Body?" Evan barked.

Goff heard, and took the steps two at a time.

"Whose body?" Evan snapped.

"A skeleton! In the landscaping!" he heard Dinkleman croak. The man was wheezing at an alarming rate and volume.

"Mr. Dinkleman, I need you to take a couple of slow, deep breaths, and explain."

"Just get—just come!" The pseudo-British accent was almost indiscernible.

Dinkleman disconnected the call, and Evan looked over at Goff. "Just run over there and see what's going on. Somebody dumped some roadkill in the yard or some other travesty."

Goff twitched his mustache and handed Evan his lunch pail.

"See it goes in the fridge," the older man said. "Tuesday's nanner pudding."

The *café con leche* was still drinkably warm when Evan finally settled in behind his desk.

His in-box looked about as full as it usually did, with nothing of extreme urgency screaming for his attention. As he flipped through call slips and little reminder notes Vi had lovingly skewed on his metal spike, a funny little scribble on the corner of a report caught his eye. It was

Paula's signature. This puzzled him for a moment, as he didn't remember requesting a report from her.

When he drew the paper out of the stack, he chuckled. Paula knew full well that he had sent her to Seaview Cove only to appease Dinkelman. He had no intention of requiring any actual results from her visit. Yet here they were, the results, written up and ready to be presented before a judge and jury if it came to that.

Evan quickly skimmed over all the perfunctory setup information about times, dates, people present and their credentials, and got straight to the meat of the report. The relevant data boiled down to the following: Three intact fingerprints had been lifted from glass shards. Two of those prints appeared smaller than a typical adult fingerprint, suggesting that it may have been left by one of the bowlers rather than one of the drinkers – assuming the bowlers were minors and the drinker or drinkers were adults. The third print was of normal size. All three prints were processed through the local database as well as through NCIC, with no matches found.

All the intact bottle mouths, nine in total, had been swabbed for DNA. There was a high likelihood that DNA was recovered with these swabs, but they had not yet been sent to the state crime lab, as they were still pending Evan's approval of the expenditure, approximately $300 per sample.

The bowling ball was a 14-pound custom drilled ball, but the manufacturer's markings had been worn off. No usable fingerprints were recovered from the bowling ball. The surface had been severely abraded by several trips down the asphalt and impacts on broken glass, rendering it unsuitable for retaining fingerprints.

The ball was not tested for DNA. Some recoverable DNA may be present in the finger holes, but the likelihood of obtaining a usable sample was low, though such tests may be attempted if the situation warranted.

At this time, the only solid lead recovered from the crime scene located at the as-yet unnamed cul-de-sac at the ass end of Seaview Cove were the names carved into the bowling ball. It appears a small pocket knife was used to deface the ball. The lack of uniformity of lettering from one name to the next tends to indicate each name was carved by a different individual. Presumably, each name was carved by the individual possessing that name.

"My recommendation, should this matter merit further investigation, would be to canvass the neighborhood in an attempt to locate a gang of kids who go by the following names: Zane, McKay, Jax, Emerson, Tatum, and Logan. Whether these suspects are male or female, your guess is as good as mine."

Evan chuckled. It might be fun to go ahead and approve the funding for the DNA tests, just to ride the ridiculousness of the situation. Those receipts would cross Quillen's desk. The councilman would then either have to eat the expense and smile about it, or he'd finally have to agree that Dinkelman was gobbling up more than his fair share of county resources. It would be a fun struggle to watch, but, Evan figured, that might be taking it one step too far. Especially since there had not been any matches on the prints. He took a long, slow pull on his coffee, then checked his wallet, wondering if the vending machine had been restocked yet this week.

When his cell rang. Goff's name popped up in the display, and Evan hit the accept button.

"Sheriff," Goff said, which was the first clue that things up at Seaview Cove were about to get a whole lot less fun. "Guess you better come on down here," he said, then added, "Looks like somebody crawled into one of Dinkleman's holes and died."

# SEVEN

EVAN ARRIVED AT the scene just ten minutes after the call. The property was one of the unfinished lots on the eastern side of the development.

Dr. Mitch Grundy, the medical examiner, hadn't shown up yet, but just about everyone else had arrived or was arriving when Evan reached Seaview Cove. He had contacted the Port St. Joe Police department, requesting help with scene control, and three of their patrol vehicles had responded.

Two ambulances and a fire engine idled along Halyard Lane. Their personnel huddled around an oddly-attired lump of man on an overburdened gurney. Evan assumed it must be Dinkelman.

Goff had related the bare bones details to Evan in their brief phone conversation. Partially skeletonized human remains had been discovered at Seaview Cove.

It had something to do with the Botanical Bandits, but Evan hadn't quite caught the connection. Meanwhile, Dinkelman's conniption had reached a level where Goff felt it expedient to request medical attention for him.

Evan rolled past the emergency vehicles, and several nearly completed but not yet occupied houses. He spotted Goff a few lots further down the road and pulled to the curb next to him. The sergeant leaned against an ornate lamppost that replicated those of 19th century London but had probably been milled in China a year ago. He was drinking what could only be horrible coffee from a local gas station. It was probably as old as the lamppost was trying to be.

"Guess this complicates things a bit," Goff said, as Evan exited his vehicle and approached. "You know, Caldwell, things have sure taken a turn for the entertaining since you showed up."

Evan shook his head. "Just show me what we're looking at."

"Carpenters arrived this morning around 7:00. They've got about three weeks to finish the interiors on these homes, and they're running about a week behind. This is according to …" he pulled a small pad from his shirt pocket and flipped it open. "Jamie Cruz, the head carpenter or foreman or what have you. Cruz says they noticed a toppled tree down there."

He lifted his chin, indicating a young bottle palm lying on its side in an otherwise neatly landscaped yard. "Saw it just about as soon as they rolled up, but felt it was in their best interest not to report it to Dink." Goff looked up and snuffled under his mustache. "As I'm sure you can appreciate."

Evan sighed. "They're behind schedule already; if they call Dinkelman about his shrubbery, they'll lose the whole day."

"Got it in one," Goff said. "Don't guess it's gonna matter now, though. Not likely gonna have a pile of people tumbling over themselves to move into a neighborhood with corpses buried under their trees."

"Corpses?" Evan asked, eyebrows raised. "With an 's'?"

"Well, not yet," Goff said, "but if this turns out like Toronto, no telling how many bodies could be out here."

"Do me a favor, Goff, don't mention Toronto to anybody else," Evan said. "As a matter of fact, don't mention it to me either."

Goff grinned. His mustache lifted and stretched like the wings of a furry seagull about to take flight. "Oh, don't worry about *me*. This story will have taken on a life of its own before you and I are done talking, if it hasn't already."

Evan had no doubt he was right. "So, the workers noticed the toppled tree around 7:00 but didn't investigate?"

Goff nodded. "Dinkelman arrived about an hour later. Jamie Cruz said he and his guys were just finishing up the trim in the upstairs bedroom there." He pointed in the direction of the two-story house across the street from the uprooted palm.

A couple of St. Joe PD officers stood there, basically to preserve the crime scene, but mostly just staring down into the hole.

"Shortly after 8:00 a.m. they heard Dink shouting," Goff continued. "They all thought they knew why and didn't bother to go look." He took a couple of healthy swallows of his coffee.

"Where are the carpenters?"

"That's them over there."

Goff pointed to the house next to the house with the suspicious landscaping. A cluster of working men stood on the little fake portico, talking to a couple of Evan's deputies.

"Jamie said when Dink shrieked, that's when they all went to the window. They thought Dink had finally taken that last lurch toward the loony bin." Goff looked up from his pad and quickly added, "According to Cruz."

"You want to go take a look with me?" Evan asked, stepping off the curb toward the scene.

"Not overmuch, no," Goff said, dropping in step behind Evan "Air's pretty still so there's no wind to stand up from."

Fresh sod had been laid over this yard within the last year. It had flourished under the tender loving care of Dinkelman's landscapers, and only a few edges of the sod squares remained discernable. Evan got his first whiff of the putrefaction as he was stepping from the asphalt to the grass. The smell intensified as he approached the crater which once cradled the palm.

The two PD officers, whom he knew only vaguely by sight, exchanged greetings and head shaking with Evan before Goff politely asked them to give him and his boss a little room.

The tree itself, lay horizontal in the lawn, pointing from the crater toward the road. A length of dirty rope was tied to its base and ran alongside its trunk, stretching several feet into the road where it terminated in a loop. Defects in the otherwise pristine lawn indicated where a vehicle had backed up into the grass, apparently in an attempt to drag the palm out of its hole. Two shovels lay abandoned on either side of the palm's root ball.

Possibly the people—and plural was indicated by the plural shovels—had tried to yank the tree partway out of the ground, then went to use their shovels to dig it up the rest of the way, Evan assumed so as not to kill the roots. Nobody stole a live tree because they wanted a dead one.

The thieves had managed to uproot the tree but hadn't wanted anything to do with what they found under it. They had been in such a hurry to be everywhere else that they hadn't taken the time to recover their tools or untie the rope. This possibly simplified Evan's job somewhat.

Evan peered over the edge of the crater and decided he didn't blame them. Botanical Bandits probably didn't get confronted by dead bodies in any kind of routine way.

The soil, augmented by who-knows-what manner of compost or manure, was black. The bones, though many shades from white, gleamed in contrast. The contrast would have been even more stark under the glare of a flashlight.

The skeleton lay on its side, legs folded up about halfway to its chest. Evan could make out only scraps of clothing, but couldn't say for sure what colors they had been. There wasn't any immediate indication of gender, but he sensed the body was probably that of a male.

At first, he thought it was missing an arm, but then he craned his neck to take a look at the partially excavated root ball. Here, the arm bones, still partially wrapped in a scrim of flesh, dangled from tendrils of the roots.

Evan turned his attention from the roots to the body. He squatted down to take a closer look and was able to make out a few more scraps of cloth around the bones in the hole. They appeared to be a thin flannel with a plaid pattern. Pajamas, maybe.

As he stood and turned to Goff, Evan saw Paula Trigg being escorted through the police perimeter by Deputies Crenshaw and Holland. Paula was in her thirties, with a dark, finely edged bob and a nick in one ear that she'd gotten by being shot while with the Miami PD. Evan had gone from Miami to Brevard County to here. Paula was a local who'd run off to Miami and then come back. Not because of the shooting; the woman was unflappable. She'd gotten the credentials she'd gone for, and come back home as soon as a job opened up.

To Goff, Evan asked, "Initial thoughts?"

"Looks like he curled up to take a nap in this convenient hole and someone planted a tree on him."

Evan gave Goff a grunt, indicating his lack of interest in the ridiculous.

"Ain't saying that's what happened, just that's what looks like happened." Goff said. "I don't figure he was a construction or landscape guy. Those aren't work clothes for one thing, and for another he kinda looks like he's been here a good bit longer than the tree. Older fella, too, looks like."

Evan looked back at the root-bound arm, hand, and finger bones. They were suggestive of gnarled age, but Goff seemed to have more confidence in his analysis than Evan could find in his own.

When Goff perceived this, he added. "I've seen hand bones that gnarly before." Looked up at him. "On my own x-rays," Goff explained, no jesting in his voice now. "Mine aren't that bad, yet, but I guess they're headed that way. Not betting the house on it, but I'd guess he was at least my age. Probably older."

Evan nodded distractedly as he stared down at their new case.

"And he's got no teeth," Goff added, "so that right there tells you something."

Evan crouched and peered into the shadow near the bottom of one edge of the crater, where the skull rested. The mandible lay where it belonged, just below the maxilla, held in place by deteriorated but not yet disintegrated tendons. No teeth appeared on either the upper or lower jaw. The angle and lighting weren't conducive to close examination.

Evan had no idea whether the teeth had been professionally removed before the man died, if they had just fallen out, or if they had been removed posthumously in an attempt to conceal the body's identity.

He stood again, distancing himself as much as possible from the odor. "I'm with you on thinking it is probably male."

"A touch too tall for your average female," Goff mused. "Especially if we're talking about an older person."

"Be nice to have an opinion more educated than our own," Evan said. He'd seen far too many dead bodies in his career, and many of them quite deteriorated, but that didn't make him an expert.

Behind them, Crenshaw exclaimed, "Phew! That's ripe."

Evan turned to see him and Deputy Holland hesitating at the edge of the lawn.

"If you don't need us up there, boss," Crenshaw said, "How 'bout Holland and I go establish a perimeter?"

Paula, coming up behind them, had set her oversized tackle box down on the road and was fishing for something in the cargo pocket of her pants. A moment later, she came up with a tube of Vicks, which she applied liberally under her nose.

"No need to come up here," Evan said to the deputies. "In fact, let's try to minimize our presence. You two maintain the perimeter. See if you can whittle it down to one PD unit in here. Beyond that, everyone else needs to stay out of Seaview for now."

Holland nodded. Crenshaw said, "Don't gotta tell me twice." And the two headed back the way they came. Paula retrieved her box and approached, reaching Evan and Goff just about the time Evan's cell buzzed. He checked the window, which informed him that Quillen had just gotten word that something was wrong with his favorite constituent.

"You going to get that?" Goff asked.

"You can have it if you like," Evan replied. When Goff didn't accept the offer, Evan silenced the phone and dropped it back in his pocket. "I'll talk to him when I've got something to tell him."

Paula nudged his elbow, offering him the Vicks.

"I'm used to it already," Evan said. "Thanks, though."

When she offered it to Goff, the sergeant declined. "Gums up the mustache," he explained.

"So," Paula asked, "What'd we find?"

"We've just started trying to figure that out," Evan said. "Has anyone called Grundy, yet?" he asked Goff.

"Called his office soon as I got off the phone with you. They said he's on vacation as of Friday night. Didn't know whether he was actually going anywhere, but I left a message anyway; told them it was urgent. Danny's already on his way back from some conference in Panama City. Should be here in twenty minutes or so." Goff glanced at his watch before going on. "Left a message on Grundy's cell, too, just to be thorough, but he doesn't answer my calls anymore anyway."

"How'd you manage that?" Paula asked, with a hint of admiration in her voice.

"Worked hard and believed in myself," Goff replied.

"Huh," Paula said, "never would have thought of that." She popped a cell out of one of her numerous pockets, tapped the screen a couple times and put it to her ear. "I'll see if I can get him." She walked to the edge of the pit and peered in. Goff and Evan joined her.

"How long do you guess he's been down there?" Evan asked either of them.

"He's still got a bit of jerky on the scalp there, and back by the ear," Goff answered. "Can't say anywhere near for certain, but I'd reckon he's been there less than a year…more than a month."

Paula gave him a disgusted look. She pulled the phone from her ear, tapped it a few more times and tried again.

"Guess I should have called it 'desiccated tissue,'" Goff said apologetically.

"'Jerky's' not the problem, Goff," she replied. "It's the sloppy science that irritates me."

Goff shook his head and chuckled. "It wasn't sloppy science, darling, it was precise speculation." He lifted the corners of his mustache at her.

She didn't seem to notice. She was focused on the remains. "Does kinda look like jerky," she muttered, then punched a third number into her phone.

Deputy Meyers approached from the backyard of the neighboring house, one hand holding a hanky over his nose. "Hey, Caldwell," he called, "where do you need me?"

"Where'd you come from?" Evan asked.

"Jumped the fence from Jacaranda Street," Meyers said. "I couldn't get in the other way; too many emergency vehicles. Also, a news van and a bunch of other civilians."

Evan grimaced. He felt the phone buzzing in his pocket. Goff's phone was bleeping, too. It was the ringtone he had assigned to Vi. Behind him, Evan heard Goff answer.

In response to Meyers' first question, Evan said, "Go on back the way you came, make sure no one else sneaks in that way until we can get this thing contained."

He heard Goff say, "Yep, I'll tell him… he'll be real excited."

Evan turned, raised an eyebrow.

"Quillen desperately needs to speak to you," Goff said.

"He said 'desperately'?" Evan asked.

"Didn't have to," Goff said. "The fact that he dared to call Vi says it all."

"Right," Evan sighed. "Right. Fine. I'll give him a call in a second," he said, fishing the phone out of his pocket. "First, what do we have here? A cold crime scene, right?"

"Pretty cold," Paula agreed.

"Which means, about the only piece of evidence worth finding is going to be the body itself, and any debris that might be in the dirt around it."

Paula and Goff nodded their agreement.

"So, we secure this yard, open the rest of the development for business as usual, and we touch nothing until the M.E. arrives," Evan said. "Speaking of which, any luck with Grundy?"

Paula shook her head in the negative. "I've called his house and his cell," she said. "But I wouldn't answer my phone, either, if I was on vacation."

"He only lives about a quarter mile back the way Meyers went," Goff said. "You can see his house from that model home the kids' been hanging around in."

"Paula, can you call Meyers, ask him to swing by Grundy's?" Evan asked.

Paula nodded and pulled out her phone. "I've got a text from Danny," she said. "ETA fifteen minutes. Texting and driving," she said, looking up. "Poor kid, he was all agitated about leaving F.A.M.E." Evan wasn't sure he wanted to know what that was.

Paula told him anyway, holding her ringing phone to her ear but away from her mouth. "Florida Association of Medical Examiners. It's their yearly conference," she said. "Grundy was supposed to go, but he found out drinks weren't covered by admission this year, so he sent Danny in his place and took his vacation instead."

"I see," he saw. "What about Kim Webber or Nick Stapleton? Isn't one of them on call while Danny and Grundy are gone?"

"Kim started her maternity leave last week. Nick is on call, but currently huddled in the fetal position in his bathtub," Paula said.

"What?" Evan had pulled his phone and had been preparing to dial Quillen. But he hesitated to hear the explanation.

"That's about as far as he dares to be away from a toilet," she elaborated. "Cryptosporidium."

When Evan didn't respond, she added, "Squiggly things that make you poop out your past, present and future."

"Delightful," Evan said.

They waited as Paula dialed Meyers and asked him to run by Grundy's.

Once she'd disconnected the call, Goff rearranged his mustache and then smiled at her. "If Grundy's watching golf in the nude on his couch, I don't want to hear about it."

Paula smiled. Her first of the day as far as Evan could tell. Goff gave her a wink, then went back to studying the bones.

Evan hit the call history on his phone. Quillen had been the last twelve calls. He heaved a sigh, then turned his back to Paula and Goff. They discussed the body while Evan dialed.

"Sheriff," Quillen's voice was abrupt, authoritative, and evidently a bit hoarse from all the screaming he had been doing while Evan ignored his calls.

"Commissioner," Evan replied.

"Dinkelman is extremely upset."

"I suspect the guy in the hole isn't too happy either."

"This is no time for irreverence. Mr. Dinkelman has invested millions in our community, Caldwell. Millions. If news gets out about this, it could ruin him. It could ruin many businesses here in this town."

"Quillen," Evan said as calmly as possible, "local carpenters found a skeleton buried under a tree."

"I am aware of that," Quillen snapped.

"Firefighters, EMS, and the neighbor kids arrived before we did," Evan went on.

"Yes?"

"So, I can give you my personal guarantee," Evan said, "that discretion isn't going to come into play today. I imagine there is at least one group of grade-school boys planning to sneak out tonight to dare each other to touch the skeleton tree."

Quillen yelled something inappropriate on the other end of the line.

Evan went on. "This was already out of our hands before it was in them. The best we can hope for now is a quick resolution."

Quillen was silent for a moment. Then he asked, "So what are you doing?"

"Well, first of all, we've been trying to get our medical examiner out here to collect the body so we can clear the scene," Evan said. "Unfortunately, nobody has been able to contact Grundy, so we're waiting on Danny, one of the interns. He'll be here shortly."

"We need to get all you law enforcement folks out of that subdivision," Quillen spat. "They're supposed to be doing some open houses today."

"I told you, we're waiting on the intern to get out here."

"Stop standing around waiting. Grab some shovels or something and get that body out of there. Now."

"Quillen, this is a crime scene, almost certainly a homicide. You get that, right?"

"Of course, I get that! What else would it be?" Quillen said. "And you're the highest-ranking law enforcement officer in the county. Can't you take pictures and whatever and give your people permission to move the thing yourself?"

"Let me make myself clear," Evan said, as calmly as he could, "The body is under the medical examiner's jurisdiction. I *cannot* touch it until he, or someone from his office, signs off on it."

A loud clattering banged out of the phone. Evan pulled it away from his ear and stared at it. Quillen had either slammed the receiver or thrown it.

Goff and Paula were watching him expectantly.

"The knowledgeable county commissioner seems to think we can just remove the body ourselves," he said quietly. "He sounds about ready to come down here and do it himself if we don't."

"I'd trust you two over Grundy, anyway," Paula said.

"I'd just about trust Quillen over Grundy," Goff said.

Evan was about to respond when he saw Meyers jogging toward them.

"No dice," Meyers reported, slightly out of breath. "The garage is locked, so I don't know if his car's in there, but I banged on the front door pretty good. No answer. Of course, that could mean he went somewhere for his vacation, or he just went to his couch and drank until he passed out."

"That guy is a walking cliché," Evan exclaimed, disgusted.

"Caldwell!" Someone, it sounded like Quillen, was shouting his name from far away. "Caldwell!"

Evan realized that his phone was still connected to the councilman's office, and the man himself had finally regained control of his own phone. He lifted the cell back to the vicinity of his ear, though not too close, and said, "Quillen? Can you hear me now?"

"I am the head of the County Commissioners!" Quillen exclaimed. "The medical examiner answers to me! You answer to me. If I say you can move the body, you darn well better be moving the body."

Evan heaved a deep, slow breath, then said, "We'll get started on that, Quillen."

There was an inarticulate grumble on the other end of the phone, then the line went dead. Evan looked at his crew in general. "Who elected this moron?"

Nobody copped to it. Evan slid his phone into his shirt pocket.

"Paula, go ahead and get some shots of the body *in situ* until Danny gets here," he said.

Paula nodded and knelt down to get a better shot.

"Now I got that Randy Travis song stuck in my head," Goff said.

"Who's Randy Travis?" Evan asked, uninterested in the answer.

"That ain't even funny," Goff said. "He was just about the biggest country star of the 80s and 90s."

"I was listening to Tears for Fears," Evan said.

"Who?"

# EIGHT

EVAN COULDN'T HELP liking Danny Coyle. The kid was twenty-six years old and smarter already than Evan was ever going to be. He was built like a stick insect, but good-looking, with dark brown hair worn kind of shaggy, and black-framed hipster glasses. The kid had the metabolism of a marmoset and spoke twice as fast as Evan was able to hear, but he grew on Evan just a little more every time they met, which, like today, was always over a dead guy.

"Oh, but this is a pickle, right?" Danny asked, peering down into the hole.

"Why?" Evan asked, squinting through the piercing sunlight.

"Well, so I've done a bunch of the extra classes and symposiums on decay and deterioration, right, but I've never actually worked on a body this old."

"Well, we're trying to get hold of your boss, but that's proving difficult," Evan said. "As you might have guessed."

"Right, yeah, vacation," Danny said, nodding sincerely. "Nonetheless, I can process our new friend, right, get him out of this yard and into the exam room, but I'm not sure I'm the best person to actually perform the autopsy. Right?"

"You don't think you can do it or you're not qualified to do it?"

Danny shook his head. "Yeah, no."

"Which?"

"Uh, so I'm not super-sure that I can do it. Like, I'd be crazy happy if you got someone else to do the actual autopsy."

"We don't have anyone else unless your drunkard boss shows up unexpectedly."

"Oh. So, conundrum, then," Danny said gravely, his dark brows coming together.

"Somewhat," Evan replied, parking his hands on his hips.

"The thing is, if book knowledge was as good as hands-on experience, I'd be sailing to French Polynesia right now, right?"

Evan could feel a circle of sweat forming in the middle of his back, and he made a mental note to pick his shirts up from the cleaners. There were six, and they were all exactly like this one.

"Look, let's get him and this scene processed, and I'll see about getting some help from Leon County, okay?"

"All righty, well, then I'll just get myself acquainted with this guy and then we'll take him back to the ME's and hope that Dr. Grundy shows up before you actually need me to *do* anything."

"That time is already here." Evan sighed. "I mean, you can do some of the work, right? You do most of the work with all of the other autopsies that come your way."

"Well, yeah, to be sure, but I might need some help with this guy, you know, because he's of a certain vintage, right?"

"Which vintage? Are we talking months, years, decades?"

"Oh, yeah, no, not decades, not here in this environment," Danny answered, pushing his glasses back up his nose. "Maybe if we were in the desert, or in like Canada, right? But not here. No, months. Maybe years, but probably months."

"Okay, it's a start," Evan said. Paula was standing across the hole, the camera resting in her palm. "Paula, you have what you need for now?"

"Yeah, I'm good," she answered. "I'll get some shots of the ground underneath him once we get him out of there."

"Okay, so let me just scurry back to the van then," Danny said. "I've gotta get some additional supplies. Okay, my smoothie, but still."

Evan stared after the kid as he gamboled back the way he'd come, knees and elbows everywhere.

"If I was ten years younger, I'd probably fall in love with that goofball," Paula said as she watched him run.

"Me, too," said Goff.

Danny ended up proving more knowledgeable than he'd expected himself to be. The body helped. The flesh on the extremities had suffered extensive decomposition, giving a first impression of a fully skeletonized body, and causing the limbs to separate easily from the rest of the remains. Danny pointed out that the head didn't detach from the neck, but the connection was more principle than reality.

The torso, though it had also suffered deterioration, was not as desiccated as the limbs. It appeared to still contain a significant portion of the viscera.

Two ambulances had answered Goff's call to assess and assist Dinkelman. Evan requested that one of the teams help excavate and transport the body, while the other removed Dinkelman from the scene. This was ostensibly for his own health, though Evan felt it would have a positive impact on the wellbeing of everyone present. The two EMT crews argued briefly over which detail was more desirable, but couldn't reach a conclusion. In the end, the matter was decided by coin toss.

Over the next few hours, the team worked to collect as much of the remains as could be differentiated from the soil and roots and assemble them on a gurney. The palm tree and all the soil that had contacted it or the body was collected on tarps, then transferred back to the climate-controlled storage building attached to the ME's office.

It was nearly two o'clock in the afternoon by the time the luckier of the two ambulance crews delivered the remains to the medical examiner's office on the other side of town.

Evan swore everyone on his team to secrecy, not only about what they had found, but also regarding the removal of the palm. He had absolutely no urge to see Dinkelman's reaction if he found out Evan had actually taken one of his freaking trees.

# NINE

AT JUST SHY of five, Evan got word from Danny that one of the Leon County MEs had zipped over from Tallahassee, conducted a preliminary exam on John Doe, and was ready to discuss his initial findings with Evan. Evan asked Goff to tag along, and they took Evan's vehicle.

"I'm not especially partial to autopsies and whatnot," Goff said, as they turned onto Memorial.

"I can think of better places to be myself," Evan said. "You don't have to come in, but I thought the ride over would give you a chance to update me on the neighborhood canvass."

"Well, I'm not gonna wait in the car like a ten-year-old," Goff sniffed. "I'm just saying I don't go out of my way to see bodies get cut and peeled and sawed and all that business."

"Understood," Evan said, trying not to smile. "So how did the canvassing work out?"

"It didn't," Goff said. "You got only twenty percent occupancy in that development, and none of 'em are on that street. But we talked to all of the residents, even the ones we had to run down at the workplace, and nobody saw anything last night. I did get one lady, lives across from the entrance, she said a few weeks ago she saw a truck come in that she didn't know, and she intended to call Dink to see if it was one of his people, but she got caught up cooking dinner, and the truck went back out like twenty minutes later, so she didn't worry about it."

"Description of the truck?"

"Wouldn't that be nice, but not really," Goff answered. "Dark pickup truck, older but not old, and she couldn't see who was inside it."

"Is that gatehouse manned?" Evan asked. "I mean, at night. I've never seen anyone in it during the day."

"Nope, they don't even have phone service out to it yet."

"Well, add that to all the other things that are unhelpful."

"Vi's got herself a spreadsheet for that."

"You know, Goff, I like you a little more every day," Evan said.

Goff looked over at him, frowning. "You're not putting the moves on me, are you?"

Evan exerted some effort in keeping a straight face. "Maybe just a little," he said.

"Well, I don't want to hurt your feelies or anything, but I have no truck with workplace romance."

To Evan, it didn't look like Goff had to work all that hard at keeping a straight face.

"It's okay, I understand," Evan said.

"The bloom fades offa that, and next thing you know, you and I are feeling all awkward at the morning muster."

Evan made a point of not looking at Goff. "Fair point."

"Besides, you don't want to excite my bride," Goff said. "She's tiny but she's powerful jealous when it comes to her man."

"Yeah, she's real frightening," Evan said dryly. Mrs. Goff looked slightly more underfed than Goff, and Evan doubted she was five feet tall.

"Don't deceive yourself; she's fierce," Goff said. "Last year, some fella over at the American Legion pinched her backside. She nailed him good, right in his fine washables."

Evan stared out the windshield and chewed his lower lip.

"He folded over like a French crepe, right there in front of God and everybody," Goff said sincerely.

Evan grinned and shook his head. "OK, you win."

Goff's face was every bit of sincere. He frowned at Evan like he didn't know what he was talking about, and then turned back to the windshield.

"He fell apart like a soggy taco," he said by way of the last word.

The Gulf County Medical Examiner's office was a squatty tan stucco building that looked like any other doctor's or accountant's office if you didn't read the sign. Evan parked in one of many empty slots in the tiny parking lot, and he and Goff went inside.

The receptionist, a middle-aged woman named Margie, showed them back to one of the three exam rooms. Waiting for them there were Danny and a much shorter, sandy-haired man who looked to be in his late forties or so. Beneath his lab coat, he wore khakis and a faded denim button-down shirt. He and Danny were standing on opposite sides of John Doe, who was lying on a stainless-steel table, still curled up on his side, but now nude.

"Oh, right, hey!" Danny said with a big grin. "Sheriff, Sgt. Goff, this is Dr. Ebersole, from Tallahassee."

Evan shook the man's hand. "Dr. Ebersole. Evan Caldwell."

"Toby," the man said, then looked at Goff, who held out a hand.

"Ruben Goff," Goff said as they shook.

"So, you're the Leon County ME," Evan said.

"One of three assistant MEs," Ebersole answered. "The Chief Medical Examiner is Nancy Trammel."

"We appreciate you coming over here to help us out," Evan said.

"No problem. Any chance to get out of Tallahassee is cool with me. It's gotten too big, man."

Ebersole turned to look at Danny, and when he did, Evan saw that he wore his hair in a tiny ponytail, which hung below a well-established bald spot.

"Well, we appreciate you and your office giving us some help," Evan said. "Danny wasn't too comfortable with handling this one on his own."

"Oh, this one's smart as a whip," Ebersole said. "He probably would have been fine."

"Yeah, no," Danny said, shaking his head.

Ebersole looked back at Evan. "So, understand that all I have for you right now is just the bare minimum findings, really. We've still got to conduct the actual post-mortem, do tissue and bone samples, toxicology, all that good stuff."

"I understand," Evan said with a nod.

"Okay, so then…you've got a male between sixty and seventy, about six-foot, give or take an inch, owing to his present posture, Caucasian, possibly Hispanic, based on skull and jaw structure. A few cursory measurements of his extremities indicate fairly large bone structure, so he was probably somewhat broad or stocky."

Ebersole reached over to a nearby stainless cart and picked up a fountain drink in a to-go cup, probably from a gas station. He took a good swallow, then put it down.

"Your guy here wore full dentures; at least, he didn't have any teeth. Professionally pulled, given the absence of roots. So dental records are going to be a no-go as far as identification."

"Wonderful," Evan said.

"Well, we still have DNA, if his DNA's in the system, and I'm also going to be taking two digits, the index and ring finger, from his left hand, back to the state lab with me. They have the most flesh remaining, and once the lab has rehydrated them so to speak, we might be able to get usable fingerprints."

"Excellent," Evan said. "Any clue as to cause of death?"

"Yes, and maybe no," Ebersole answered. "Xrays showed a triangular piece of metal lodged against his spine, between L-3 and L-4 of the lumbar vertebra." He glanced over at Evan and Goff. "The lower back. Could be a broken knife tip, but I won't know until I go in and get it. So, it could be he was stabbed to death, but with the condition of the skin over that area, I can't find an entry wound with the naked eye. I'll know more once I get a closer look."

"Any idea how long he's been dead?" Evan asked.

"Again, we'll need to do some tissue analysis to get a firmer idea, but based on eyeballing the remains, and my knowledge of the soil and ambient temperatures here in the Panhandle, I'd put it between twelve and eighteen months. Of course, he might not have been buried right away, and seventeen hundred other variables, but it's probably going to be in that range, yeah. I'll know more in a couple of days."

"Okay," Evan said. "When are you going back to Tallahassee with the, uh, fingers?"

"Later today. I'm gonna run them and our tissue and bone samples to our lab, and I'll call you as soon as I have more info for you. Probably tomorrow." He picked up his cup and took another drink. "I know Coke's terrible for you, but I drink like six of these a day ever since I gave up weed."

He looked up at Danny and smiled, but Danny looked like he'd been slapped, and glanced nervously over at Evan.

"Cool it, kid, it's a joke," Ebersole said, smiling. "I haven't smoked weed since med school."

Danny nodded vigorously. "Oh, right, right, yeah," he said enthusiastically. Then he looked over at Evan. "Not that I ever smoked weed. Well, I tried it once in high school, but it freaked me out, right? I thought my parrot was trying to kill me. Yeah. I spazzed."

Evan couldn't imagine the kid spazzing, as spazzing was his resting state.

"I find that hard to imagine, kid," Ebersole said, echoing Evan's thought. "You talk so fast, every time you say something, I feel like I ought to be square dancing."

Evan held up a hand. "I don't care what you did in high school, Danny," he reassured him. "We're good."

Danny laughed. "Yeah, right? I get that sometimes." He looked at Evan. "Hey, let me go get the printout of the prelim, just so you have it."

"Thanks, Danny," Evan said.

Ebersole watched Danny gallop through the door to the back office, then he looked at Evan. "I like this kid. And you've got a righteous little town, here. If your ME slipped off to Costa Rica or signed himself into rehab or something, I'm unencumbered and happy to relocate."

"We just might take you up on that," Evan said.

A few minutes later, Evan and Goff stood by the Pilot, both front doors open, as they waited for the interior to cool off.

"He's on the flaky side, maybe, but I wouldn't mind him taking Grundy's place," Goff said.

"No, he's definitely better than Grundy."

"He's vertical for one thing," Goff said, as he slipped into the passenger seat.

# TEN

WEDNESDAY MORNING WAS a confluence of absurdities. Evan had to explain to his crew that the case of the Botanical Bandito had not only been elevated to the status of a real case, but it was also their top priority. It was possible that the uprooted palm had been chosen at random, as they assumed had all the prior missing trees. But, it was also possible that this particular tree had been uprooted on purpose to draw attention to the secret it hid. If that was the case, then the tree thieves likely had some information about how the body ended up under there.

Crenshaw suggested sending out BOLOs for the missing trees. The suggestion garnered a smattering of chuckles and a long-suffering sigh from Holland.

"Actually, Crenshaw, that's not a bad idea," Evan said, then turned to Goff. "Sergeant, put Crenshaw and his partner down to work up BOLOs on the missing palms."

Across the room, Meyers groaned.

Crenshaw said, "No, Boss, I was just…"

"You were joking. He's not," Goff talked over Crenshaw. "Between us and the PD, we know these missing trees are gone. The PD, and Dinkelman himself, probably, have checked every plot of dirt in PSJ and can verify that none of these plants reside within the city limits. You guys know what these plants look like. The city cops are intimately familiar with what these plants look like. But the police in whatever place these plants got off to won't know one shrub from another, and won't care, neither. If we're to find the guys who dug up that body, we need to find Dinkelman's missing shrubs, and to do that, we're gonna have to tell the neighboring jurisdictions what we're looking for."

Some heads nodded. Some eyes rolled.

Evan went on to detail the remainder of the assignments and priorities for the day, none of which registered high on the excitement scale. Searching through missing persons files for Gulf and neighboring counties for men in their 60's to 70's, compiling a list of all employees and contractors who worked in Seaview Cove over the last twelve months, narrowing these down to those who would have had access to that particular plot around the estimated time of death, and interviewing all the current residents of the Cove about suspicious activity.

"One other thing," Evan added, trying not to sound as reluctant as he felt, "we need to find our Medical Examiner."

This brought more laughter than Crenshaw's comment about the plant BOLO.

"Don't worry, he'll turn up eventually," Meyers said. "He always does."

"I'm not worried about him," Evan said. "I just need him to show up and sign off on this autopsy. Ebersole called this morning and said since he is the ME, he's going to have to sin off on any test results or findings before we could use them to get a search or arrest warrant. If any of you know where he might be or who might be able to contact him, let me know."

"You want us to add his picture to the plant BOLOs?" Crenshaw asked.

"Let's keep the Grundy issue in-house for now," Evan said.

"And if you have any more great ideas," Meyers said to Crenshaw, "keep 'em to yourself."

This brought a few chuckles and murmurs of agreement throughout the muster room.

Evan said, "Anyone, other than Crenshaw, have anything to add?" When no one did, he closed with, "Goff has your assignments."

Thirty minutes later, Evan found himself headed west on 98 towards Panama City, with Deputy Holland riding shotgun. He'd have to ask Goff about that later, when the entire shift wasn't there watching. Evan was the obvious pick for the Panama City assignment, but Deputy Holland would not have been Evan's first choice. The deputy probably would not have elected to ride with Evan, either, if it had been up to him. Evan could have over-ridden Goff's assignment, but not without fueling the office gossip about a feud between him and Holland. He wondered if Goff had set him up intentionally, maybe as payback for sending Goff on the Dinkelman call, or if it had just been luck of the draw. Either way, it made for an awkward morning.

Before leaving, Evan had contacted the Panama City interagency liaison to let them know his intentions and to request any help they could provide. Officer Cal Rochester, who Evan knew from a prior case, had been assigned to help them. Rochester had compiled a list of half a dozen unlisted lawn services, guys who ran lawn mowing and tree trimming businesses out of their garage or backyard, but who had no business license on file. Dinkelman had also provided a list of suspects who he believed may have been responsible for his vanish-ing shrubberies.

The first stop on their tour was a tiny, but neatly kept, cottage on the side of Highway 98. Its yard glowed a bright green in the morning sun and the foundation was neatly lined with flowers and ornamental shrubs. A wood plank hung beneath the mailbox with the word "Mowing," hand painted, followed by a local phone number, no area code.

The business owner, a man named Shane Arps, said he never did any planting of trees, just trimming and husk removal. The type of trees Dinkelman had lost, some of them anyway, would stick out like a busted thumb. If you knew what you were looking for, anyhow.

He promised to keep his eyes open and call if he saw any busted thumbs, but also figured there'd be more of that sort of thing in the populated areas, nodding down the road toward Panama City.

They visited a couple businesses in Mexico Beach, with similar results, and were about to head for Panama City when Holland, who hadn't said two words to Evan so far, nodded to a turnoff. The narrow road curved into the pine forest, disappearing behind the trees and under their dense shadows.

"Cracker Bowl's down there," Holland said.

"Cracker Bowl?" Evan asked.

"Grundy likes to drink there most Friday nights," Holland said. "Might be worth your time to ask if they've seen him."

Evan peered down the unmarked lane, then looked back at Holland. "No sign?" he asked.

The deputy shrugged. "It's a place for locals. If you know where it is, you're welcome," he said. "I don't guess you'd have found it on your own."

Evan wasn't sure how to respond, but he also felt a bit happier about Goff's decision to pair him with Holland. If he was headed into a backwoods, locals only-type establishment, it might be good to have a local with him.

"Your type of place?" Evan asked, preparing to turn down the shady, unmarked road.

"I like it fine," Holland said. "But it wouldn't do no good to go now. They don't open 'till five on weekdays."

Evan took a quick glance at the dash clock, just a hair past eleven. "We'll hit it on the way back, then."

Holland nodded, but said no more.

They were halfway to Panama City when Evan got a call from Toby Ebersole. They were still working on fingerprints, but Ebersole could tell Evan that stabbing didn't appear to be the cause of death. There were no entry wounds to the skin in the area of the man's lower spine, and he'd found that flesh and scar tissue had grown around the triangular object, enough of it to indicate that it had probably been there for many years and that it was possible the man had been advised not to have it removed surgically, since it might have done more harm than leaving it there.

Dried residue in the stomach had shown both sedatives and Flexeril were in his system at the time of death, but Ebersole couldn't say yet that they had contributed to that death.

Ebersole also let Evan know that Danny had suggested tracing the fragment of metal found in the dead man's spine. There were some very deteriorated markings on one side of the fragment, but the lab was still working on it.

Evan hung up and looked over at Holland. "Well, that's more than Grundy's given us."

He dialed Goff's number and relayed the information to the sergeant.

He advised Goff that the number one priority was to get an ID on their victim, but if fingerprints were going to help at all, they were going to help later. Until then, they would need to focus on finding out who had access to that yard from eighteen months to a year ago? Who planted the tree that stood over the man's grave and when?

Evan told Goff to have a couple people get employment and subcontractor records for the time in question, and task the rest with running background checks and conducting interviews with those people.

It didn't escape Evan's notice, the fact that they'd been focused on who was taking stuff *out* of Dinkelman's yards, and now they needed to find out who was putting things *in* them. He would have appreciated the irony, but he wasn't really having that kind of day.

# ELEVEN

BY THE TIME the sun had burned all the blue out of the late spring sky, Sheriff Caldwell and Deputy Holland had stopped at a couple dozen businesses dealing in landscaping or other plant-related concerns. What they learned amounted to an entire day's worth of nothing. Their most enlightening encounter turned out to be the outfit Dinkelman had been most concerned with, the one he had insisted Evan stake out.

Happy Garden was more of a lawn and garden supply shop than a landscaping business, though they did have a small smattering of rose bushes and shrubs for sale. The owner, a lanky Latino who introduced himself as Chevy, laughed heartily when Evan mentioned Dinkelman's name – then offered his condolences. The man moved like a willow but when Evan shook his hand, it felt like a rock.

"He hates me," Chevy said, the hint of a chuckle still evident in his speech. "I worked for him many years, but the man, he is an insufferable bore. As soon as I saved enough to buy this place, I told him so." Chevy looked at the rose tree he had been pruning, yellow at its base igniting to a vibrant orange at the tips of its petals, then back up to Evan and Holland. "I guess I shouldn't have said it in front of everybody, but I think they all knew it already."

"Yeah," Holland said. "He doesn't go out of his way to hide it."

Chevy's eyes twinkled. He clipped a newly-blossoming rosebud, and handed it to Evan. "You give this to Dinkelman. Tell him there is no hard feelings. Also, tell him I don't take his trees. And I don't buy his trees from the guys who steal them. I have enough dirt on my hands from honest work; no need to dirty my soul as well, eh?"

"These 'guys that steal them,'" Evan asked, "you ever met these guys? They ever try to sell you plants they might have stolen from Dinkelman, or anyone else?"

"Oh, sure," Chevy said with a dismissive flap of his hand. "Every couple month these guys come by. I always run them off though. Those types are bad news. They steal from George because George had dealings with them before, that's my guess; they saw what he had, then later they took it." Chevy shrugged. "You play soccer with the devil, you get hoofprints in your shin guards."

"Would you have names for these guys?" Evan asked. "Or any ideas where we could find them?"

Chevy looked confused for a minute, then his lips broke open in a gleaming smile. "Oh, no, Sheriff. I don't think you understand." He chuckled easily again. "It's not the same guys. It's different guys every time. Once Chevy runs 'em off," he tapped his chest with his fingertips, "they don't come back."

"Wait, what?" Holland asked.

"I make it very plain," Chevy said. "I tell them they come back and I call the ambulance."

"Not the police?"

"They'll need an ambulance more than they'll need the police, if they come back," Chevy said, still smiling.

The charisma in his smile was powerful, the kind of power that could be terrifying if he used that smile when he wasn't happy. Evan could believe a would-be hustler would hustle his goods somewhere else after a single encounter with that smile.

"So, you're telling me it wasn't just one set of guys stealing Dinkelman's trees?" Evan asked. "You're saying several different individuals have been doing this same stupid con?"

"How long you been a sheriff, Sheriff?" Chevy smiled and shook his head. "These tweakers and junkies, they take anything they can sell. Kid got killed – electrocuted – last year trying to steal wires off his neighbor's house to sell for scrap metal."

"I remember that," Evan said.

"So, yeah, one meth-head who still has two brain cells to rub together gets this bright idea about turning one of Dinkelman's trees into a baggie of powder." Chevy wasn't smiling now. "It worked out for that guy, so prob'ly every other scab-faced waste from here to Tate's Hell has tried it, or plans to, when they run low on blow."

Chevy's anger didn't seem to suit him. Evan guessed the man had more than a passing encounter with the drug culture, and whatever that experience was, it had been deeply painful. He looked at his notepad, giving the man a moment to cool. Then he said, "Chevy, I really appreciate you being so cooperative. I want to go back over what you've told us, just to make sure I understand everything."

Chevy nodded and gestured for Evan to continue.

"You're saying that you've had direct contact with the people who stole trees out of Seaview Cove?"

Chevy nodded.

"And each time it was a different person or group of people?"

Chevy nodded again.

"And you know that some, or all, of these people are habitual drug users?"

"I couldn't testify to it," Chevy clarified, "but I know it in my heart. You look at them, and you just know."

"Sure," Evan nodded. "Listen, I'm not much concerned with Dinkelman, or his trees, but it is vital that I find the guys who were in Seaview Cove last night…" Chevy started shaking his head, but Evan persisted, "anything at all you can tell me, first names, general descriptions, type of vehicle?"

"I would help you, Sheriff, if I could," Chevy said, still shaking his head, "but I work very hard to put those things out of my mind. When I get a spina in my finger, I pull it out and forget about it. I don't waste time finding out what plant poked me, right?"

"When was the last time someone offered to sell you stolen plants?" Holland asked.

"Oh, a week?" Chevy said, turning his attention to Holland. "Two weeks? I don't remember."

"Any chance they might show up on your security cameras?" Evan asked.

Chevy's eyes brightened, then fell again. "Maybe they did," he said, "but we only keep the pictures a few days, then they are gone, recorded over."

"I see," Evan said. He drew a card from his pocket and handed it to the man. "You've been very helpful. Please, if you think of anything at all that might help us identify any one of these guys, please give me a call."

Chevy took the card. "I will call if I think of anything."

"And you're sure you never bought any of the trees these boys were selling?" Holland asked. "Not even once?"

Chevy laughed openly again, like he did when they first met. He pointed a finger at Holland, but spoke to Evan. "This one's like a bulldog, no?"

"You could say that," Evan said.

"I don't like Dinkelman, and I don't like his tastes in plants," Chevy said. "There is nothing he has that I want. Nor do I want to have anything more to do with his business, either for good or ill." After a pause, he added, "No, I did not accept a single plant that was stolen from him, or anyone else."

Evan thanked him again, as did Holland, though his was more obligatory than sincere. Then the two headed to the next shop on their itinerary. They kept at it until four-thirty that afternoon, with expectations sagging lower from one stop to the next. No one had any information to offer beyond what Chevy had provided. They would have headed home earlier, except Evan wanted to check in at the bar Holland had pointed out in Mexico beach. If he could get a line on his Medical Examiner, at least the trip wouldn't be a complete waste.

# TWELVE

THE DAY HAD started somewhere beyond the far side of normal. Evan guessed he had no right to expect it would end any different. With the sun hanging low over the gulf, and the gulf reflecting its orange glare at savage angles, the shadowy gravel road leading to Grundy's Friday night hangout felt even less inviting than it had that morning.

The old pines flanking Highway 98 were leftovers from a tree farm grown for the St. Joe Company's paper mill that had closed back in the late nineties. They had been planted, acre upon acre, in uniform rows, like a gigantic field of corn. The orange sunset cast them in a strangely disquieting light. The black hole where the gravel road pierced this fiery façade was downright creepy.

Evan expressed none of these feelings to Holland as he turned into the gap between the pines. Inside the stand of trees, as the Pilot's tires crunched along the well-maintained gravel road, the last remnants of the day's light strobed in diminishing slashes through the unnervingly even tree rows.

Throughout the day, Evan had made one or two ill-fated attempts at small talk. Holland, to his credit, had also made an attempt, asking Evan if he'd ever done any hunting out here, but that conversation was relatively short-lived. They now rode in silence through the dusty auburn twilight.

Cracker Bowl, from the outside, looked about as identical to what Evan imagined as possible. He guessed he could have provided a nearly perfect description of the place before he had even seen it. An extravagant neon sign hovered over a tin roof, proclaiming to anyone who didn't know that this was, indeed, Cracker Bowl. Humbler neons advertising various beers hung in the only two windows, flanking a double door. The building was low-slung, as Evan had anticipated, but it seemed unusually long. The gravel lot could hold maybe a couple dozen pickup trucks, though only four currently occupied it.

Evan followed Holland through the doors, at Holland's recommendation, and at first glance, found the interior to be as close a match to his expectations as the outside had been. A bar, a few tables, a few booths, pool and darts at one end of the long room, a small dance floor and cramped stage for live music directly across from the bar.

It was the rack of ugly leather shoes at the far end that clued Evan in to Cracker Bowl's peculiarity among back-woods bars. As he ventured deeper into the space, Evan saw the reason for the building's unusual length. Beyond the bar and all its expected furnishings, four lanes of hardwood stretched into the distance.

"They've got a bowling alley back there," Evan said, surprised, and maybe a bit mystified. Realizing this, he was able to make better sense of the signs on the wall, the most cryptic of which read, "Do Not ask Mindy to set your pins."

Holland, who had already made it halfway to the bar, turned with a look of startled disgust. "Why else would they've called it Cracker Bowl?"

"Right," Evan said, with a single chuckle, "Of course." He moved across the dim room to catch up with his deputy.

"You gone a bit too far," a gruff and gravelly voice barked from behind the bar. "Got all the necessary licenses and permits and up-to-date inspection stickers, posted right there in the entryway, Sheriff. No call for you to be coming all the way in here." The man was big and ugly, with glossy black hair that probably came from Seminole blood, but built broad and thick as any hillbilly linebacker.

Evan had hoped Holland would make introductions and facilitate the conversation, but the barman had ignored the deputy, as if he hadn't even seen him, and he had known, on sight, who Evan was. Evan felt that falling back on Holland at this point would show a flavor of weakness that wouldn't be tolerated here, and would probably come across as an insult to the barman.

"I got certificates, I got stamps, I got stickers," the big guy continued, thrusting a hard, thick finger back towards the entryway. "I got an ominous domminous diddly doo from the pope himself. Whatever it is you need to figure out, it's posted right up there."

"I don't think what I'm looking for is up there." Evan had made a quick sweep of the room as he entered and counted six patrons scattered throughout the establishment. They were all now keenly interested in the outcome of this conversation.

"Well, it sure ain't back here, whatever it is," the man said, lifting his chin. His chest rose as he inhaled, and he seemed to grow two inches taller. "And if you *think* it's back here, you ain't gonna like finding out you're wrong."

"Jerald," Holland said, with a longsuffering sigh.

The barman – Jerald, apparently – cracked a smile that was just as ugly as the face that wore it, but the two together made the whole man, not beautiful exactly, but somehow comforting to look at.

"Patrick!" Jerald exclaimed. "Are you with him? What you doing dragging this nice city boy into a dive like this?"

Holland moved up beside Evan at the bar. Evan noticed that all the others in the room seemed to have already forgotten they existed.

"Cut the crap, Jerald," Holland said, "it's been a long day."

"Longer for this guy," Jerald said, nodding to Evan, "if he's been stuck with you."

From one of the shadowy corners, somebody laughed out loud.

"I don't even know why I come in here," Holland griped.

"I do," Jerald said, with mischief playing on his face, "but I'll keep it to myself if you make your business brief."

"I don't want to be here right now any more than you want me," Holland snapped. "We just need to know if you've seen Grundy."

"Sure, Mitch is usually here from about six till close, almost every Friday," Jerald said. "Sometimes I joke that it's guys like him keeping me in business." He turned to Evan, smiling wide, "But most of the time, it ain't no joke," and ended with a wink.

Evan couldn't help but smile. He figured Jerald used that line every chance he got, but Evan couldn't blame him. "Was he here last Friday?"

"I just told you he's here every Friday night," the barman said, but not with any hostility.

Holland opened his mouth to say something, but Evan reached over and touched Holland's elbow, halting whatever indignant response Holland might be working on; a response that would lead to an inevitable, prolonged, circular conversation that would no doubt amuse Jerald and his vast number of patrons, but would likely not produce any useful information.

"So he was here," Evan said.

"Nope."

Evan thought about arresting the man for thinking he was cute.

Jerald's lips pressed tightly together and quivered slightly. Evan could see the man trying to decide whether to keep playing with them or shoot straight. Finally, he said, "He's here most Fridays. Don't guess I saw him this last Friday though." He thought for a moment, then said, "No, not this Friday. Is he in trouble or something?"

"He's gonna be in a heap of trouble," Holland said, "if he doesn't have one hell of a good excuse."

"He's on vacation, but we need him to help us with something. Unfortunately, we haven't been able to get hold of him," Evan said.

"Well, shoot, if I'd known it was something like that, I wouldn't have hassled you," Jerald said.

By the look on the man's face now, Evan guessed that might even be true. "Do you have any idea where he might have gone?"

"Not a clue," Jerald said, shaking his head. "I saw him just about every week for years, passed a few words like I do with everybody, but I don't know anything about who he was when he wasn't here."

"Who did he hang out with when he *was* here?" Evan asked. "Anybody who might know a bit more about where he could be?"

"Well, there's four or five guys that were on his bowling team," Jerald said. "We have a pretty loose league, you know, teams form up and fall apart, one month to the next. But those guys, they didn't know where he was either, now that you mention it. They were all kinda pissed at him because he was supposed to be here, you know. They were expecting him."

He pulled a tattered leather accounting book from under the cash register and flopped it open on the bar. He flipped through several pages until he found what he was looking for, then pointed to a list of names in one column. Several of the names had been scratched out and replaced with others. Some were accompanied by phone numbers. Most were not.

"These here are Grundy's team," Jerald said. "You can copy down their names and numbers, but don't tell 'em where you got 'em."

The team names, and the names of their members, took up only a few of the many columns. In the remaining space, Evan saw numbers and dollar signs, splits and spreads, figures indicating wagers made, monies collected, winnings paid, debts outstanding. He didn't guess any of the permits, stickers or certificates up front covered this piece of Cracker Bowl's action, but that was a matter for another day. Maybe.

For now, he neatly copied the three names and two numbers Jerald indicated into his notebook, and thanked the man. He promised not to reveal his source, although he figured nobody, including Jerald, really cared. Every one of the others in the bar could have overheard their conversation.

"Look," Jerald said, "I feel like an ass for hassling you earlier. How 'bout a round on the house?"

Holland looked over to Evan, "It's after five," he said, "we're off duty."

"You're still in uniform," Evan said, tapping his notepad on the bar and stepping away.

"You're not," Jerald countered, pulling a large glass stein off an overhead shelf. "I insist."

"Rain check," Evan said. "Thank you, again." He nodded Holland to the door, then headed that way himself.

"I'm taking that as a promise, Sheriff Caldwell," Jerald called after them.

Evan stopped to see Hannah, then ran into The Pig to see what looked good for dinner. He was tired and out of sorts and didn't want to go to a lot of trouble, but he was also hungry and feeling the need for a little nutritional therapy. He ended up splurging on a few enormous sea scallops.

Evan was relieved to find that Plutes hadn't inflicted any special damage on the boat that day. An African violet was knocked over on one of the tables in the salon, its dirt spread out like ripples in a pond. It was the same African violet that had been overturned at least ten times, and Evan was less than amused that it kept thriving, when Evan couldn't keep a philodendron alive.

He cleaned up the mess, then fired up the grill out on the sundeck, put his square cast iron grill pan inside, and closed the lid. Evan could live on seafood, but he could live without having the smell inside for days.

He got out of his work clothes and put on some cargo shorts and a white tee shirt. He luxuriated in being barefoot as he walked from his stateroom, across the salon, and down into the U-shaped galley. He grabbed the small package of scallops, some asparagus, butter, and lemon, and went out onto the sundeck. Plutes had wandered out there earlier, and Evan found him perched atop one of the starboard-side lockers, tail barely twitching.

"It might interest you to know," Evan said, "That dinner cost me twenty-five dollars. So, I'd appreciate it if you'd show a little gratitude and refrain from yakking it up on my stateroom floor."

Apparently, it did not interest Plutes to know; the cat gave Evan one slow blink and then turned to gaze out over the darkening marina.

Evan oiled and seasoned the asparagus and threw them directly on the grill. Then he lightly seasoned the scallops and carefully placed them in the cast iron grill pan.

"Leave it," he said to Plutes as he went inside to grab a plate and some flatware for himself, and a saucer for the idiot. Plutes was right where he'd left him when Evan got back. He stood at the grill, worrying over the scallops and wielding a pair of tongs for the moment when it would be time to turn them. The time finally came, and turn them he finally did, then he dashed into the galley for a bottle of water and arrived back at the grill just in time to remove the scallops from the heat.

He placed five on his own plate and one on Plutes's. If he liked it, he could have another, unless Evan ate it first.

"You'll find, if you set aside your clear and annoying biases, that sea scallops are far superior to bay scallops; I don't care what any of these Panhandle people say."

Evan placed the saucer on the locker in front of Plutes, who sniffed at it tentatively.

"I would cut it for you to cool it off," Evan said, "But it's essential for you to notice the perfect sear. The caramelization is half the thing."

Evan put the asparagus on his plate, squeezed some lemon over everything, and sat down at the rattan table.

"Well?" he asked the cat.

Plutes sniffed again, then batted it onto the floor. Evan was about to voice his outrage when Plutes jumped down, sniffed a few more times, then gave it a lick.

"Right?" Evan asked.

Plutes blinked at him a couple of times, then jumped back onto the locker and settled himself into what Evan called his white bread formation. Evan tossed his fork down onto his plate and stood.

"Do you have any idea at all what a luxurious item this is?" He parked his hands on his hips for a moment as he peered down at the scallop. "Are you honestly going to tell me that gravel you eat is preferable to a perfectly-cooked scallop?"

Plutes was apparently not going to assert anything at all. He stared at some point near Evan's knees.

Evan contemplated picking the scallop up and putting it on his plate, but then he thought about the number of people who had walked on the sundeck in their sweaty socks, and the frequency with which Plutes used the litter box, tucked inside a deck locker that had had its door removed, and then sashayed across the sundeck with his furry, litter-y, urine-soaked cat feet.

Evan sighed in disgust, picked up the scallop, and tossed it overboard. He watched as it landed with a tiny plop, and was immediately scooped up by a seagull who'd been relaxing on a weathered pile.

Evan looked over at Plutes. "That seagull was much less of a jackass than you are, and everybody knows gulls are the jackasses of the sea."

# THIRTEEN

THURSDAY MORNING DAWNED hot and muggy, particularly muggy for April, and Evan felt like he needed another shower by the time he got to the office. He was running late because Plutes had taken it upon himself to drag Evan's left black loafer under the bed, and Evan would rather be shot than wear his brown loafers with the navy suit he'd already put on. Once he'd found the shoe, remonstrated the cat and made his to-go coffee, he was already five minutes late. Fortunately, the Sheriff's Office was less than five minutes from the marina. So was everything else.

Evan decided to forgo checking in with Vi, and went straight to the conference room. Everyone on duty was already assembled, with Goff in his usual spot to the right of Evan's chair at the head of the long, oval table. He was quietly consuming what looked like a homemade blueberry muffin, a paper napkin tucked into his collar, while everyone else talked over each other about some fishing tournament coming up that weekend. The conversation died down as Evan closed the door behind him.

"Good morning," Evan said to the room at large and got several greetings back.

"You're nine minutes late," Goff said, flicking a crumb from his mustache. "We're not used to it. I was mulling over asking Vi to send out a BOLO on you."

"The cat," Evan said simply as he sat down.

"Naturally," Goff replied.

"All right, let's get right down to the priority business of the day," Evan said to the room. "We can recap other cases and progress afterwards." He pulled out his notepad. "Okay. Yesterday's neighborhood canvassing seems to bear out Chevy Munoz's statement that there is more than one individual or group stealing landscaping around here. Unfortunately, the few people you guys have been able to attach names to are all in the clear for Tuesday's excavation. Two of them are down the hall in the jail, and one of them, Cody Taylor, got himself run over in the Walmart parking lot in Panama City five days ago."

"Who gets run over in a Walmart parking lot?" Meyers asked. "How fast could the car have been going?"

"Faster than Cody Taylor, looks like," Goff said as he took the napkin from his collar.

"In any case," Evan continued, "Those guys are a dead end. We have to keep in mind, too, that the guys who stole the trees from Dinkelman probably aren't the guys who buried our John Doe. We're just hoping one of those guys knows who did, or noticed when that ground got dug up and replaced, because Dinkelman doesn't."

"For all we know, that guy's been there since before Dinkelman started building that place," Holland offered.

"True." Evan took a sip of his *café con leche*. "But we can't go back indefinitely, so let's assume somebody thought a new construction site with a lot of fresh land-scaping was a good place to dump a body. We ought to also assume, and by assume I mean hope, that it was somebody who had easy access to the site. So, let's focus our attention on current and past employees, subcontractors, even delivery people, anybody with a legitimate reason to be on the property at some point."

"Are we dropping the tweakers?" Meyers asked.

"No, but they're going to be harder to identify and find. And honestly, if I was a tweaker at a brand-new construction site, I wouldn't be stealing trees, I'd be going for the copper, wouldn't you?"

"Well, Bo," Goff said.

"Bo what?"

"Bo Middleton," Goff answered, at the same time as a few of the other guys. "Got himself fried to hell and yonder last year, ripping copper wire out of his next-door neighbor's remodel. Copper thievery saw a sudden drop after that, and we got more stolen guardrails, street signs, and whatnot. Tweakers are a superstitious lot."

"Well, when everything and everyone is out to get you, including crossing guards and Bigfoot, it's not really superstition," Evan said dryly. "In any event, I think our time is better spent on looking at people with legitimate access to the development, including homeowners. That and finding out who our John Doe is." Evan took another swallow of his coffee. "Once the ME gets back with some info from the fingers, we'll be overjoyed, but for now what we have is what we have. Missing persons is a no go. No males in the right age range reported missing during the right time range, as much as we've been able to pin that down."

Evan flipped a page in his notebook. "Meyers, you and Holland talk to Dinkelman and his office manager, what was her name?"

"Barbara Finch," Deputy Crenshaw answered. "She's my second cousin on my mama's side."

"Okay, well, then why don't you and Cooper do this then? You guys talk to Dink and your aunt, get a list of every single person, past or present, with legitimate reason to be on the job site since they broke ground in September 2018."

"Okay," Crenshaw said.

Evan looked over at Meyers and Holland. "You guys run some background checks on anybody over eighteen that owns a house or lives in a house in Seaview Cove. Come to think of it, find out if any of them employs a landscaping service, somebody to mow their lawn, whatever."

"Gotcha," Holland said.

"Run the backgrounds first, so you know who you're talking to, then go out and talk to them. If they're at work, go there."

Meyers nodded and Evan looked around the room at the remaining half dozen deputies. "The rest of you keep going on the tweakers. Maybe we'll get uncharacteristically lucky."

He checked the date on his watch. "Tomorrow is Mitch Grundy's last day of vacation. When he gets back from wherever he's been, maybe he'll meander into the exam room and help us find out more about this guy, including how he got so dead."

He turned to Amy Peterson, one of two female deputies on his staff. Paula was the other. "Amy, anything fruitful from your conversations with Grundy's bowling buddies?"

"No," she answered, shaking her head. "Nobody's seen him. Guess we're just gonna have to wait."

"What a pain in the ass this guy is." Evan stood. "Okay, let's get going. Goff, can you come back to the office with me?"

Once Goff cleared his place and adjusted his sagging utility belt, he and Evan walked down the hall toward

Evan's office. When they entered the reception area, they found Vi, resplendent in teal Bermuda shorts and a shirt covered in flamingoes, watering one of the aloe plants on her desk. She looked up at them over her bifocals and grimaced. But then, she only had two facial expressions that Evan knew of: grimace and frown.

"Mr. Caldwell," she said, and it sounded like an admonishment. "I have twenty-two days of paid leave accrued, and I will be constrained to take at least half of them if George Dinkelman calls here one more time."

"I'm sorry, Vi," Evan said.

"The man even had the hubris to call me on my cell phone last night during *Downton Abbey.*"

"How did he get your cell number?" Evan asked sharply.

"From that strutting capon Quillen, who deems it necessary to have the cell numbers of everyone employed by the county," Vi answered. She shook her head disgustedly as she spoke, the rhinestone lanyard of her glasses jingling against her silver hoops.

"I'll talk to him, Vi," Evan said, hoping to placate someone that had probably never been placated in her life. "Any messages?"

"Nothing I haven't already handled." Vi sat down in her desk chair with a sigh. "Please be reminded that I have an appointment to get Mr. Fawlty neutered at 3 pm, so someone will have to take calls." She frowned at

Goff, who shifted from one foot to the other. "Perhaps you can forward calls to Olive Oyl's desk."

"I told her to quit calling me that," Goff muttered.

"Vi, don't call names," Evan said. "Can you give Sgt. Goff that list of nursing homes in the area?"

"What do you think I need that for?" Goff asked.

Evan gave him a look. "I was thinking, this guy was in his pajamas. Maybe he wandered off from a nursing home or some facility like that."

"Wouldn't they have filed a missing persons?"

"You would think, but we're working with nothing at this point."

A few minutes later, Evan closed his office door behind him, slid off his blazer, hung it on the back of his chair, and sat down. He tried to come up with several important things to do before he did the one he needed to do, but he came up empty. He drained his *café con leche* and picked up the desk phone receiver.

There were six officers total with the Wewahitchka Police Department if you counted the command staff, so Evan wasn't all that surprised when Chief Nathan Beckett himself answered the phone.

"Bigtime!" Beckett said, in a tone that was somehow both hearty and dismissive. "I was wondering when you'd get around to calling out here."

As much as Evan tried to *dis*like Nathan Beckett, he had developed a grudging respect for the guy, and maybe even a little genuine liking. Beckett tried to play the backwoods lawman, kicking the dirt around with his steel-toed boot, but every now and then he used big words in the proper context, and every now and then he showed some genuine character.

"Looks like today's the day," Evan replied, then after a pause, "What exactly did you expect me to be calling about?"

"I got your BOLO, man," Beckett said, and Evan could hear the grin. "I've been policing a long time, Hollywood; can't say I've ever seen a BOLO for a tree before." He paused. "They don't typically make themselves that hard to find. Not in my experience, anyway."

"These ones had help," Evan said.

"Let me save you some time, Sheriff. They're not in Wewa. We don't have any fancy trees, and if one showed up, I'd notice. We don't even have a landscaping company out this way, just yard work, and we've got kids to do that."

"Good to know," Evan said. "I've actually got something else I'd like to discuss with you."

"Well, if it isn't upscale trees," Beckett chuckled, "it's got to be that precocious little lawyer you got for Tommy Morrow."

"Ms. Abernathy," Evan said, "and I had nothing to do with her being selected to represent Mr. Morrow."

"She's a hot little firecracker, isn't she?" Beckett asked, then whistled lightly through his teeth. "I hear she'd like you to light her fuse."

"I'm married," Evan said, flatly.

"That's right," Beckett said, "That's true. But that torch ain't gonna get any lighter." Evan detected a hint of sincerity in the other man's voice. "Just something to consider."

Evan had no interest in considering any aspect of his marriage at this particular moment, and certainly not over the phone with the Wewa Chief of Police. Without reference to Beckett's sage advice, Evan moved directly to the purpose of the call.

"Abernathy wants to put on a show, use Tommy as a soapbox so she can get all kinds of TV time," he said. "She plans to plaster mud all over my office, and yours, so she can run for a council seat next year."

"You figured that out all on your own, did you?" Beckett asked.

"I don't think it's a big secret," Evan said.

"You calling to warn me or ask for help?"

"I'm calling because she asked me to help her," Evan said. "She offered to keep me out of it if I help her throw you under the bus."

There was no immediate reply, to the point that Evan wondered if the line had gone dead. Silence wasn't Beckett's style. Then, it was broken by a long, low chuckle, followed by a drawn-out *whew*.

When Beckett finally made actual words, they were, "I don't even know where to start, Bigtime."

Evan waited. At least now he had the man's attention.

"Not sure how it's done over there in the Florida Dangle, but around here, cops don't cozy up with the defense to go after other cops," Beckett said. "Even if the defense in question is hot and handy."

Evan sighed. "Look, she's hoping to launch her political career off this case, but if she does, it's going to make a bad situation a whole lot worse, right?"

"Already covered that," Beckett said tersely. "Now I'm trying to figure what it is she thinks you've got on me."

"On the other side of the table, the DA is hoping to score points by slam-dunking Tommy into an electric chair, and neither you nor I think that's right."

"Listen, Hollywood," Beckett said. "I just rolled into the station, I mean, right before you called. Emma sent me off with a nice hot cherry pie I was planning on savoring over a phone call with my high-rolling colleague, and now you bring up Tommy Morrow and the chair? This pie's gonna be cold before I'll be able to eat it."

"I'm sorry about your pie, Beckett," Evan said with as much remorse as he could muster. Which was none. "I'm just wondering how you intend to handle Abernathy."

"Any way she'll let me," he chuckled, but then his voice dropped. "Look, Caldwell, Tommy killed Hutch. He shouldn't have done it. It sucks that he did. It sucks that he's gonna end up paying the tab for the both of them." There was a muffled *thunk* at the other end of the line, which Evan guessed must have been Beckett's boot dropping from his desk to the floor. "This ain't a Disney flick, Bigtime. Sometimes the princess marries the evil magician and the wide-eyed underdog gets hit by a car."

Evan wondered what Emma had put in that pie.

Beckett continued, "Abernathy is your problem. Morrow? Yep, he's your problem, too. It's your name on the case file. It's your picture in all the papers. You tell her whatever you want about me. As far as I remember, you and I played it straight. There isn't any bus for you to throw me under. And if there is, it's you going under, not me."

"What if we both go under?" Evan asked. "And take DA Chimes and Abernathy with us?"

Another muffled *thunk*, Beckett's other boot coming off the table. Another low chuckle, but this sounded about one degree warmer. "Evan, my man, for someone as averse to politics as you claim to be, you sure have a lot of potential for it."

"No, thanks," Evan said. "I didn't even want *this* job."

"I bet that sentiment grows a little each day," Beckett replied.

"A little bit." Evan sighed. "Look, Beckett, apparently, Tommy recollected enough of his arrest to tell Abernathy he thought you removed his work glove for him, without cause. 'Without cause' being her words, according to the paperwork she gave me. She'd like me to back that up."

"And?"

"And I have no intention of doing that," Evan answered. "We both know Tommy doesn't deserve the chair, and I'm going to testify to that effect inasmuch as is possible, but he did commit a murder. And somebody that malleable who was willing to kill when told to, that person needed to be off the street."

"And people think we'll never be close friends," Beckett said.

"Look, I'm trying to figure out how to get her off my neck, and as it happens, yours. Any help from your corner would be appreciated. Maybe you can come up with some ideas for getting this lady off our backs."

"Aside from tossing her into the nearest sinkhole?"

"Aside from that, yes."

"I'm just a small-town cop, my man, that sounds like a job for an elected official."

"I wasn't elected, I was shoved," Evan said tightly.

"All the same," Beckett said.

Evan thought those words had a comma behind them and waited to hear the rest, but the rest was just the quiet click of a disconnected call. Evan dropped the receiver back into the cradle, got to his feet, and went out for a smoke. Maybe he didn't like Nathan Beckett as much as he thought he was starting to. If he wanted to get jerked around, he could go home to the cat.

# FOURTEEN

EVAN'S DAY WENT from mildly annoying to truly bad when he looked up from his table outside at the Dockside Grill and found himself sitting in the rather bulky shadow of County Commissioner James Quillen.

Evan considered the Dockside Grill his front porch, as it belonged to the Port St. Joe Marina and he could see his boat from the side deck. As his front porch, Evan considered the Dockside Grill to be private, though he'd brought Goff to lunch there more than once. But he liked Goff. Quillen, he didn't like.

"Caldwell, we need to speak," Quillen said, his heat-reddened jowls shaking.

"Why is that?" Evan asked, already mourning his lunch.

Quillen yanked out the chair across from Evan and lowered himself into it. Then he crossed his arms on the table like he was settling in for a good talking-to, and Evan wished that soft-shelled crabs made better weapons than they did.

"I've been on the phone half the day with George Dinkelman," Quillen said.

"You have my condolences."

"This isn't playtime, Caldwell," Quillen said sharply. "Dinkelman is a very valuable constituent."

"Aren't we all?" Evan asked with sincerity. "I vote."

"Don't get smart with me today, Caldwell. I'm in no mood. Dinkelman is not only a vital supporter, but he's also a very valuable addition to this county's economy."

"This case is getting my full attention, Quillen, so I'm not sure why you sound like you're blaming me for Dinkelman's crisis."

"Your job isn't just to solve this case, it's to do it as quickly and as discretely as possible while keeping Dinkelman happy."

"Actually, that last bit isn't my job at all—"

"It is if you want to get reelected next year!"

"I can't get reelected if I wasn't elected the first time, and I grow less interested in keeping this position every day," Evan said evenly. "I've been with one Sheriff's Office or another for almost twenty years, and I hope to retire from the Sheriff's Office at some point, but I couldn't care less about being the sheriff, so don't hang that title in front of me; it's not the carrot you seem to think it is."

As Evan spoke, Quillen got redder and redder before turning white. Evan hoped it was because he'd stopped breathing, but he was quickly disappointed.

"If you want to continue with the Gulf County Sheriff's Office in *any* capacity, and continue getting the health insurance you most certainly depend on for your wife's care, you will stop acting like you're doing me and this county a favor by being here," the commissioner said.

"What is it that you want me to do, really?" Evan asked.

"You need to be a little more helpful to Ms. Abernathy for one thing," the older man answered.

"Do you know how unusual it is for a sheriff or any law enforcement officer to be told to be more helpful to a defense attorney?" Evan asked. "Because your request is bordering on the ridiculous."

Quillen opened his mouth to speak, then seemed to draw the thought back in. Evan watched him visibly change tack. When he spoke again, his voice was lower, his tone more polite.

"Listen, Evan," the man said. "We're on the same team here. We're supposed to be helping each other, not hindering each other."

"Which means what?" Evan said. He saw an artery in Quillen's neck pulse.

"Which means we need to work together to keep Dinkelman happy, keep him supportive of our mission as men who serve this county and keep his company right here in Gulf County and on the Gulf County tax books. You get what I'm saying?"

"Commissioner, my lunch is getting cold, and as you said, I have a case to close quickly and discreetly," Evan said. "So maybe you could bottom-line this for me."

"Okay, bottom line," Quillen said, trying and failing to sound pleasant. "Dinkelman's a big fan of Abby Abernathy; he wants to see her elected to the county commissioners, and the Tommy Morrow case can do that for her. She's got Dinkelman all on her side about it, and he's putting the pressure on me."

"Tommy Morrow is a developmentally-disabled kid who deserves leniency, in my opinion, but he did commit murder," Evan said.

"I know that," Quillen said a bit snippily. "We all know that. But like you said, he's not in complete control of his faculties. It would help him out if you helped her out."

"Ms. Abernathy all but tried to blackmail me earlier this week, Quillen," Evan said. "And by the way, everything she tried to use can be rebutted, refuted and wrapped up in a nice little lawsuit with her name on it."

"Suing Ms. Abernathy would be counter to our purposes," Quillen said.

"No, it would be counter to yours." Evan stood, dropping his napkin onto his cold and now-soggy soft-shelled crab basket. "Mr. Quillen—"

"Commissioner Quillen."

"Commissioner Quillen," Evan said in his best stab at a tolerant tone. "Yes, you are, in fact, my boss, as are the rest of the commissioners. However, we've covered this ground before. I didn't ask for the position of sheriff, in fact, I tried to decline it. Don't threaten me with the loss of my job; I'll find another one."

Evan didn't wait to hear what Quillen was gearing up to say. He turned and walked out to the parking lot, where the midday sun had grown unseasonably brutal and iridescent waves curled up from the asphalt.

Given Abby Abernathy's tactics in dealing with him, he had to wonder what she had or thought she had on Dinkelman. Or Quillen, for that matter. Whatever it might be, he couldn't help hoping that it was true, and that she'd play that hand sometime soon.

Evan headed south, in the general direction of Seaview Cove. He pulled up Deputy Meyers' number on his cell and hit the call button.

"Boss?" Meyers answered.

"Hey, Meyers," Evan said. "How's the day treating you?"

"Can't complain too much more than I normally do," Meyers said. "Goff and I are having some burritos at Pepper's. What can I do for you?"

"You went by Grundy's house the other day, right? The morning we dug up the body at Seaview?"

"Yeah," Meyers said, "but he wasn't there."

"He doesn't seem to be anywhere else, either," Evan said.

"You starting to get worried about him?"

Evan said, "His absence is becoming a problem. Do me a favor, guys, and swing by his place."

"Welfare check?" Meyers asked.

"I guess that works as well as anything else I might call it. I'm headed to Seaview after I stop for some coffee, so just give me a call and let me know what's up. If he's there, I might run over there and yank him out of his socks."

"Sure, no problem," Meyers said. "He lives in the subdivision right past Seaview. You can see the back of Grundy's house from that lot where the kids have been messing around. White house with turquoise awnings. Wheelchair ramps at the front and back."

"Wheelchair ramps?"

"Yeah, they were there when he bought the place. He said he was leaving them there in case he needed them when he got old, but it's probably just that a ramp is easier than steps when you're drunk as all get out."

"Right. Makes perfect sense," Evan said. "I'll talk to you in a bit."

Evan was pulling away from the No-Name Café with his coffee when not Meyers but Goff called him back.

"Boss, reckon you better drive past Seaview and come on over here to Grundy's," Goff said.

"Why?" Evan asked, already irritated.

"Feller's dead. Ripe, too," Goff said. "He's been here a good bit."

"Aw, crap," Evan said. "This guy is *such* a pain in the ass. You think it's a heart attack?"

"Nope, it's a homicide."

It took Evan a second to process that, unbelieving that his day had degenerated to this level of bad.

"Are you telling me somebody killed our ME?" he asked finally.

"Smote him good."

Grundy's house was at the far back of a neighborhood that ended at the city limit line. A split-rail fence separated these homes from the homes of Seaview Cove on the entrance side, but in the back, where Grundy's house was, there was actually an access road from Grundy's neighborhood to Dinkelman's development. Grundy's place sat on a corner lot, the back of his house, where the garage was, facing the access road. The yard was decorated by one lonely and ragged palm. Evan thought it could have used a landscaper.

Goff and Meyers were waiting in the driveway that led from the street to the garage. Meyers looked a little shaken. Goff just looked inconvenienced. Evan greeted them, then at Goff's invitation, followed them up the wheelchair ramp to an open sliding glass door. On the way up, Evan looked over his shoulder. Yeah, he could see the house where the kids had been up to no good, not two hundred yards away.

They hadn't even made it halfway up the wheelchair ramp before Evan got a nose-full of what they were there for. He had worked enough death investigations to know what week-old-dead-guy smelled like.

"You didn't notice any odor on Monday?" Evan asked Meyers.

"Nah, my nose was already full of dead guy smell," Meyers said. "That's the main reason I came over here, to get away from the stink. And I didn't come around back, I just knocked on the front door and walked up the driveway to see if the car was here, but the garage was closed and locked.

"Guess this complicates our schedule this week," Meyers said. "At least Dinkelman will cheer up a bit."

"Did he have an issue with Grundy?" Evan asked, eyebrow raised.

Meyers laughed, backing back down the ramp. "No, not that I know of. Prob'ly the only civil servant in the county that guy didn't have an issue with," he said. "But a murdered medical examiner will take the spotlight off the body under his tree."

Evan looked at Goff as they reached the back deck. He wasn't in a hurry to go inside. The smell got more powerful with every step.

"So how do you know it's a homicide?" he asked Goff.

"His head's caved in," Goff answered. "Also, if that old cuss was gonna die any other way, he'd have done it a long time ago."

It took twenty-five minutes after Evan's calls for the team to arrive. Danny Coyle and Paula Trigg, as well as two Port St. Joe City police officers responded.

Mitch Grundy's back deck led, via a sliding glass door to a laundry room. To the left, open to the laundry room, was a kitchen. Straight ahead was a dining room. Mitch Grundy was slumped against a wall in the laundry room, opposite an open closet door. His legs were splayed in front of him, one leg in the open closet across from him, the other crumpled behind him in a way that people usually don't want their legs to go.

A reusable cloth shopping bag, adorned with a cheery grinning pig, spilled its contents across his body and the surrounding floor – a stainless steel flask, a white hand towel, shoelaces, and a magazine with a close-up photo of an elderly woman selling something on its back cover, either Viagra or adult diapers, Evan couldn't tell which. The dead doctor wore a shiny red and yellow polyester polo shirt, and he had a grapefruit-sized dent in his skull that Evan hadn't noticed the last time he had seen him.

Danny tried to help Paula set up her lights, as Paula tried to avoid stepping on Danny. Outside, the PD officers were stringing up crime tape.

Goff materialized beside Evan. "You figure he's been here all week?"

"It's looking that way," Evan said. "Last time anyone saw him was when he left work on Friday. Obviously, he made it here, but I doubt he's been anywhere else."

Evan looked from Goff to Meyers and back again.

"Was the door unlocked?" he asked.

"Not just unlocked," Meyers answered. "Wide open."

They stared down at the body for a moment.

"I'm pretty sure this is the first time Grundy ever beat us to a crime scene," Goff said.

Evan turned a reproachful glance at Goff, but the old sergeant didn't seem to notice; he stood with his fists planted on his nonexistent hips, surveying the scene.

"Hey, boss?" Meyers called, from deeper in the house. Something in his voice told Evan the dead doctor wasn't the end of his worries. "I think you might want to come have a look at this."

Goff gave Evan a mustache-veiled smirk, and Evan blew out a sigh. Danny, who had been trying to help Paula, much to her dismay, also looked to Evan after hearing Meyers' voice.

"Let's go have a look," Evan said, then nodded for Goff and Danny to follow.

They found Meyers in a spare bedroom that had been turned into a museum of sorts. Perhaps it was thought of as more of an art gallery.

One wall was covered in framed degrees and certificates, as well as several pictures of Grundy shaking hands with other doctors and a few politicians. In one of them, he and Quillen stood together for a photo op at what looked to be some kind of county function.

Rows of shelves had been mounted on the other three walls. Perched on these shelves, as prim and proper as a boys' choir at a sacred service, sat nearly three dozen Cabbage Patch dolls. Each doll had a lock of hair, unmistakably human, clipped into the yarn on its head. A little placard sat beside each, identifying it by first and last name. The rest of the room was empty, except for a worn swivel chair at its center.

"What for crap sake is *this*, now?" Evan asked in a strained voice.

Danny moved past him into the room. "No, this is not a good thing." He walked further into the room as Goff and Paula crowded behind Evan. Danny lifted one of the name placards in his gloved hand. He swallowed, hard. "Actually, it's super bad."

He reached out to the next doll on the shelf and read the placard there.

"Maribelle Watts," he said, a tremor in his voice. "We did her autopsy last fall. Poor woman, couldn't keep the weight off, died of heart failure. The date is right here."

He reversed the card, though Evan was too far away to read it. Then he indicated the salt-and-pepper curl clipped into the yarn on the doll's head. "I can pretty much guarantee that is Maribelle's hair."

He looked back at Evan, eyes wide, "This is really super bad."

# FIFTEEN

EVAN, GOFF, AND Paula stood just inside the doorway, wondering at the macabre collection, pondering the solitary swivel chair at the center of the otherwise unfurnished room, for several minutes. Danny moved from Maribelle Watts to the next doll, closely examining, but not touching, the name tag. Then he moved to the next. After the fourth, he moved a bit more quickly. After the tenth, he reported, to whoever was within earshot, "Some of these I don't know, but the dates on those are from before my time. But, they're all his...uh, clients."

"Clients?" Goff asked, unbelieving.

Danny swallowed, then nodded. "All autopsies we've done," he said. "He has them all here."

He stepped closer to one of the shelves and peered down. "Uh, so, he also has their photos. There are photos of the deceased under the dolls."

"Okay, this is way too creepy," Paula said. Which was saying a lot, coming from a crime scene investigator. "I'm going back to the body with the concave skull."

Goff just whistled, low.

The shelves were white, and the dolls had held Evan's attention to the point that he hadn't noticed the photos each doll sat upon. Danny had said he didn't know all of the people in question, but Evan agreed with the kid's assumption: the photos must be of the decedents.

"Why?" Danny asked, so quietly that he might have been talking to himself.

That question was one Evan didn't even want to consider right now. In fact, the room was full of questions he didn't want to consider, now or ever. But what he wanted didn't really seem to matter much to anyone anymore. It would all come to light soon enough, and apparently, it was his lot to be the one to bring about that revelation. He might not have a choice in that, but he did still have the ability to control the timing. For now, the priority was the death investigation. Grundy's heinous Cabbage Patch/autopsy fixation room would have to wait, which didn't hurt Evan's feelings much at all.

"Danny," Evan said, "Back out of there. We're closing this up until…"

He didn't know what the end of that sentence was supposed to be, so he left it.

"Danny," Evan said, "this goes for you too, Goff. And Meyers…where'd Meyers go?"

"Out here in the hall, boss," Meyers said. "It was getting stuffy in there."

"Listen, all of you, this is confidential, very sensitive information," Evan said. "Nobody discusses this with anybody until we understand what is going on here."

"Uh, yep," Goff muttered. He was peering at another photo.

Danny nodded, his eyes wide and watery.

Meyers said, "I hear you, boss."

"Let's close this room up for now," Evan said, herding Danny toward the door.

Back in the laundry room, Paula called, "Ready for you Danny."

Normally, that would have put more of a spring in his step than was already present, but Danny's energy level had dropped all the way down to that of a normal human. He turned and headed toward her call.

"Hey, Danny," Evan said, "Are you up for this?"

"Kinda gotta be," he said, as a single word. "I mean, one's pregnant, one's sick, and this one's dead, right?"

"Look, Danny," Evan said, taking the kid by his upper arm. "If you are *not* up for it, your first responsibility is to tell me that."

Danny stared back at him, unblinking.

"I would rather wait for Toby Ebersole to run back here from Leon if you're not confident in your ability to work this scene."

Evan watched him, nodding just slightly, giving Danny the okay to walk away if that's what he needed. "Having to work someone you know is bad enough, but that," Evan nodded back to the doll room, "That's probably going to give me nightmares. Just say the word and I'll bring someone else in."

"Danny," Paula called again, a bit impatiently.

"Yeah, no," he said quietly. "I can do it."

Evan watched him until he was around the corner – the kid's spine straightened and his shoulders un-slumped as he went – then Evan returned to the doll room, this time focusing on the wall of photos.

From the hall, Meyers asked Evan, "Do you believe him?"

"If he didn't," Goff answered, "he wouldn't have let him go." After a pause, the sergeant asked, "How are *you* doing, Meyers?"

"I'm doing just fine out here," Meyers said. "And I agree with the boss. It's a good idea to keep that door closed for now."

Goff looked the man up and down, and then nodded. "Nothing gets by you, does it?" When Meyers didn't reply, Goff said, "You're on comms, and scene control. Make sure nobody comes in the house unless they're needed."

Meyers nodded, "Got it."

"And Meyers," Goff added, "Try not to find any more clues."

"I'll do my best," Meyers said, heading for the door.

Goff walked back into the room and looked at Evan.

"What do you actually know about this guy, Grundy?" Evan asked.

"Not this much, I can tell you that." Goff sighed and rubbed at his mustache. "Well, he ain't a local. Folks from around here don't…you know."

Goff gestured vaguely at the worn chair at the center of the room. Then cleared his throat and went on. "Our people aren't like this is all I'm saying."

"Not local," Evan said. "When did he show up in town?"

"Oh, maybe ten years back? No…it was the year my bride and I took a cruise to the Bahamas, the first time I had doings with Grundy, so…" Goff counted on his fingers while looking at the ceiling, "I guess it'd be going on twelve years now."

Evan thought maybe he should count Goff's fingers to figure out how he got to twelve, but weirder things were afoot. He'd add it to his to-do list for later. For now, he asked, "Does he have any relatives in town? Or anywhere he came from?"

"I heard he came from Arkansas," Goff said. "He might have people there, but I've never heard of him having family around here."

"Well, let's find out."

"You think he might have got up to this kind of thing back in Arkansas, and that's why he came here?"

"I would be surprised if he didn't, but I doubt he was caught," Evan said. "MEs have to go through an FBI background check."

"Good point."

Evan bent closer to one of the frames hanging on the wall, a letter written in crayon. It said, 'Thank you for taking good care of my grandma.' "You know what all this looks like to me?" Evan asked.

"Motive," Goff said.

"Motive," Evan agreed. "When Paula is done out there, I want her to set this up and process it as a crime scene. There are a lot of secrets in this room. If we can figure out which one of them got Grundy killed, that'll put us a lot closer to figuring out who killed him."

"It's your show, Sheriff," Goff said. He had stepped away from the wall, almost to the center of the room where the chair was, and was standing, arms crossed, back swayed, taking in the whole scene. "But, it's late. Grundy ain't getting any deader, and all this will still be here tomorrow."

Evan's initial impulse was to protest, but he'd known Goff long enough to not take his counsel lightly. The shock in Danny's eyes and the distress in Meyers' argued in Goff's favor as well. He thought for a moment, checked his watch, then realized that he was in agreement with his sergeant.

He nodded and said, "Peters is Midnights sergeant. I'll have him meet you here to relieve you, and I'll give him these same orders. As soon as they have transported the body, this whole place goes on lockdown. Nobody opens this door until Paula gets a crack at it tomorrow morning. I want a sergeant at the door and a deputy outside between now and then."

"We're actually inside city limits here," Goff reminded him. "Want me to ask PD?"

"Yeah, go ahead, but it's a homicide investigation," Evan said, "If PD had found him, they would have called us to investigate anyway. We'll just save them a step."

# SIXTEEN

THE FOLLOWING MORNING, Evan was just getting in his car when his phone rang. It was Danny.

"Hey, Danny," Evan said when he answered.

"Oh, hey," Danny said, sounding, as always, like he'd just jumped out of his chair. "So, I have some early findings for you on Dr. Grundy, right? Is this a good time? I tried to wait for, you know, a decent hour."

"This is fine, but what time did you go in?"

"Oh, right, so I never left," the kid answered. From his tone, he was awaiting some kind of admonishment.

"You worked all night?"

"Sure, right. I was kind of anxious to see what was what, you know? And then, uh, get him out of the shop. As it were."

"I get it," Evan said. He started the car to get the air going. It wasn't even eight and the unseasonal and unforgiving April heat was already well in gear.

"You're cool with me doing the whole shebang, right? Or do you want me to call Dr. Ebersole? He likes us."

"Danny, how many autopsies has Grundy signed off on for my cases since I've been here?"

"Uh, well, allowing for mathematical or recollection error due to lack of sleep and an atypical consumption of Red Bull, I think it's four."

"And who performed those autopsies?"

"Uh…"

"Right. So, yes, I'm perfectly fine with you doing it, as long as whoever your boss is, is okay with it."

"That would be Dr. Grundy, just recently deceased."

"Okay, so who's his boss?"

"Right, so I think that would be the county. Like, the county commissioners would be my guess. They have to approve all intern hires, so…yeah, them."

"They would be fine with it, too, but we'll just ask Ebersole if he'll review it and sign off on it for us, okay?"

"Right, so like with Grundy."

"Almost exactly," Evan said dryly. "So, what do you have for me?"

"Oh, sure. So, cause of death, which, like, isn't going to sneak up on you, is blunt force trauma to the head. Like, super blunt and really forceful, right?"

"Okay, any ideas on the weapon?"

"Something without any projections or anything, right, because it didn't actually break the skin," Danny said. "And wielded with some real intention, like, whoever conked him meant business. They weren't just trying to knock him out or anything. But I'm still working on weapon ideas, right, because early days and whatnot."

"Okay, what else do we know so far?" Evan asked.

"Well, at this stage of decomp, it gets harder to give a narrow time frame for TOD, but we can safely say late Friday to late Saturday."

"Was he drunk?"

"Uh, so, by forty-eight hours after death, you can't get an even reasonable idea of BAC," Danny answered. "But I've never seen him sober."

Evan huffed in disgust and disbelief. "Okay, I know that everybody and their brother knew he was a drunk, but are you telling me nobody cared if he showed up to work snockered?"

"Oh, yeah, no," the kid answered. "He never came in reeking and stumbling and the like. But, my dad was a raging alcoholic in every sense of the word 'raging' and when you grow up with somebody like that, you learn to tell when somebody's had a glass of wine even, right? So, yeah, he looked and acted straight, and vodka was his alcohol of choice anyway, right, not too smelly, but I could tell. And so, yeah, he was drunk every time I've seen him."

"Okay. Well, there were enough empty and half-empty bottles in his trash to indicate he was probably drunk. Either that or he hadn't taken his trash out in a long time," Evan added dryly.

"Too true."

"Anything else?"

"Not yet, no," Danny replied. "Uh, I'm working on that weapon, though."

"Any defensive wounds?"

"Not unless he was defending himself against the M&M guys," Danny answered. "He had chocolate all over his hands."

Evan hadn't eaten the night before. The decomp smell and the creepy dolls at Grundy's had cured any appetite he might have had, or might have today. That greasy feeling in his stomach and halfway up his throat was still with him at noon, and on his way back to the office after a status meeting with Quillen and his band of merry commissioners, hunger had not yet reasserted itself to the point that lunch interested him. Instead, Evan smoked an extra cigarette on the way.

The AC in the Sheriff's Office was cold enough, after the heat of the outdoors, to fog up his sunglasses in 6.2 seconds. He took them off, nodded a greeting to the deputy at the front desk, and headed down the carpeted hall.

No one was around in the bullpen, but a door at the back of the room stood open to the back parking lot. There had been no prisoners in the holding cells when he'd left this morning, so he wasn't worried they would escape, but all the cool air was making a break for it.

He was about to return to the front desk to ask what was going on when an odd squeaking drew his attention. He watched Deputy Holland walk backward through the open door, pulling a rolling dolly stacked high with evidence boxes. Each box had "Grundy" written in large letters with black marker. The dolly's wheels wept as the deputy trundled it through the bullpen to the evidence room. The scowl on Holland's face made his usual scowl look cheery. He must have seen Evan standing there, but made no effort to acknowledge him.

As Evan moved toward the open door, Paula came through, pushing a similar stack of boxes on a similar dolly. He saw the crime scene van parked just outside the door, its back open. Three additional deputies were working to unload boxes and transfer them to lockup.

"This is all from Grundy?" Evan asked, following her dolly as she rolled by.

Paula laid into him with a withering stare. "I am a crime scene investigator, not a freaking reality show host," she said coldly, shouldering past him. "I'd appreciate it if you keep that in mind."

He smelled cigarette smoke on her breath, which he hadn't noticed last night.

"This," she grabbed a Jordache shoe box and rattled it at him, "contains approximately one-point-three pounds of fingernail clippings." She raised both eyebrows at him aggressively. "Do you know how many fingernails you'd have to clip to get one-point-three pounds of them?"

Evan did not.

"I swear, Caldwell, one more like this and I'm going back to Miami. I'll take cartel paybacks and gang initiations any day."

The light in the room dimmed slightly and Evan turned to see Deputy Crenshaw standing in the doorway, three large boxes in his arms. He looked unsure as to whether it was safe to proceed. A second deputy stepped up behind him, similarly burdened.

"Give us a minute," Evan said, and Crenshaw seemed happy to comply. To Paula, Evan said in a low voice, "I asked you to keep a lid on this. How much did these guys see?"

"All they saw was boxes," she said. "They saw the girl moving boxes and felt compelled to intervene."

"I think their eagerness to help comes more from a desire to avoid their tedious assignments than rampant chauvinism," Evan said.

Deputy Holland hollered from inside the evidence locker, "Don't worry, she didn't show me none of your TOP-SECRET EVIDENCE."

Paula rolled her eyes up at the ceiling and tried for an angry exhalation of disgust. Halfway through, she cracked and let half a smile slip by her. "He is such an ass, sometimes."

"I'll go talk to him."

"No, don't."

Evan looked at her until she looked him in the eye.

"What?" she asked, her lip curling.

"I know you can handle your boxes just fine. But if what's in them," he pointed at the box of toenails, "If that's freaking you out it's okay to say so."

"I can do it," she said, with more certainty than defiance, "I just don't want to. I don't get off on this whack job weirdo crap like some techs do. This isn't what I'm here for. There's no crime to solve, no bad guy to catch, no benefit to the community, just some old creep with strange fascinations that I have absolutely no interest in understanding. There's nothing in this for me but a whole lot of cringing and paperwork."

Evan nodded. Understanding Grundy's collection might give them a clue to his killer, and Paula knew that, but he could relate to her desire for Grundy's psyche to remain a mystery. "Not much I can do about the paperwork," he said, "but I'm willing to cringe with you if it helps."

"Is it safe to come out now?" Holland called, still in the evidence locker.

"I think what would help most is if you found something else for *him* to do," she said. "Also, if you have any of those Marlboros on you, can I bum one? I'm taking a break from quitting today."

That was something Evan understood far too well. He handed her the half pack that had been riding around in his sports coat pocket. "Take a break from the boxes, while you're at it. I'll go have a word with Holland."

"Deputy," Evan addressed Holland as he entered the lockup.

The deputy was leaning against a wall of steel shelves, his arms folded, legs crossed at the ankle, but his scowl seemed to have wandered off.

"Sheriff," Holland replied, a sly smile teasing the corners of his mouth.

"You seemed a bit agitated out there," Evan said. "You have something on your mind?"

"I think you know what I, and the whole rest of the department, are 'agitated' about," Holland said, and Evan noticed his tone had calmed and was much less ragged than his resting gripe voice, which he found a bit alarming. "But in case you haven't caught on yet, Sheriff, we're all on the same team here. Holding out on us." He thumped one of the sealed Grundy boxes. Something shifted inside the box and it made Evan's gut twitch. "That tells us you don't trust us, and that crap don't play here."

"I'm sorry you feel that way, Holland. I have my reasons for keeping this under wraps for now, and none of them have anything to do with trust."

"Look, Sheriff," Holland said. The rancor had left his voice; the mischief had left his smile, "You want to keep us in the dark, that's fine. You like to lone-wolf it, be my guest. But let me clue you in to something you'd probably never have figured out on your own. See that scuffed up bowling ball that I noticed over there while you were out in the hall with your secrets?"

He lifted his chin at the shelf directly behind Evan's head, the shelf he'd been looking at when Evan came in. "That's Grundy's ball. That's the ball he'd have taken out to Cracker Bowl Friday night, if he'd'a gone."

"Are you serious?"

"I saw him with it all the time; it's uglier than sin, but he polished and paraded that thing like it was his Super Bowl ring. So, what's it doing here?"

"That's the ball that Dinkelman's vandals used to bust up all those beer bottles on his property."

"Well, you might want someone you trust to go find out why Dinkelman's vandals had Grundy's ball."

# SEVENTEEN

HOLLAND HAD NO doubts, he had assured Evan. The ball was Grundy's.

It had been found just a few hundred yards from Grundy's home within a day of his death, and suddenly, how it got there was the most important question on the table.

Evan asked Paula to drop everything and reexamine the ball, for reals this time, to which she replied, "I did it for reals the first time," but agreed to have a second look. Whether it was because she expected to find anything or just to get away from the dolls, Evan didn't know, but either answer was acceptable under the circumstances.

He felt that he and Holland had done enough bonding for one month, so he grabbed Crenshaw to ride along. Crenshaw seemed to get along with Dinkelman just fine, anyway.

They took Evan's vehicle and headed for Seaview Cove, with Paula's original report on the Cove Bowlers in hand. He called Dinkelman, *en route*, and asked him to meet them there, baiting him with the pseudo-truth that they had a new lead on the bowling bandits.

Dinkelman got almost romantic about that news and excitedly agreed to meet them at the "scene of the crime."

He beat them there. When Evan and Crenshaw arrived, Dinkelman was pacing around his silver Mercedes like a man in the waiting room of a maternity ward. Before Evan was out of the car, Dinkelman was coming for him.

"What have you got, Caldwell?" he asked in his weird, not-quite-British accent.

"Good afternoon, George," Evan said, extending his hand to shake.

Dinkelman shook it, but distractedly. His eyes were fixated on the file in Evan's other hand, Paula's report. "What have you got?" he repeated as if that was the proper response to Evan's "good afternoon."

"George," Evan started, "are you aware that Dr. Mitch Grundy was found dead at his home last night?"

"That wasn't in Seaview Cove," Dinkelman responded immediately. His chest puffed out. His excited tone turned suspicious, and his voice went from gruff to gruffer. "That has absolutely nothing to do with my development." Then his eyes grew shrewd, "You told me this was about the vandals. What are you playing at, Caldwell?"

"The ball that you found right here on this lot belonged to Dr. Grundy. He lived right over there." Evan turned and pointed at the back of Grundy's house, just a few hundred yards away. He turned back to Dinkelman and watched his eyes to make sure he was following the conversation.

"We suspect foul play in Dr. Grundy's death, so it is incredibly important that we figure out how his bowling b—"

"Another murder!" Dinkelman shouted. "Is this not exactly what I told you would happen? I did, didn't I? I told you, you lie around and ignore the little crimes," he put 'little' in air quotes with his stubby fingers. "You ignore the petty crimes, and pretty soon? Pretty soon, what have you got? Huh?" He demanded, "What have you got? Murder! Murder is what you got!"

"Mr. Dinkelman—"

"And not just one murder, *two* murders!" he shouted.

His sausage-like fingers were now splayed and thrust forward at Evan to emphasize that there had, in fact, been two murders. He reminded Evan of Richard Nixon in his famous pose, but less good-looking.

"Because you would not take me seriously," Dinkelman went on. "Because you laughed at me! Maybe next time you'll listen. Do you think?"

"But not in Seaview," Crenshaw offered.

"What?" Dinkelman wheeled around, but when he saw it was Crenshaw, he said, "Oh, hello, Jimmy," in a surprisingly friendly tone.

"Two murders, yes," Crenshaw said, "But only one in Seaview."

"You don't want it to get out that the murder rate in Seaview Cove has doubled in one week," Caldwell said, smiling at his deputy. He had time to lose the smile before Dinkelman spun back around to him.

"You will report nothing of the kind," Dinkelman hissed, invading Evan's space. "That doctor did not die in my development!"

"Right," Evan started.

"And if you had done your job in the first place—"

"George!" Evan snapped. He'd had quite enough of Dinkelman's tantrums. The day had been too long already, and this man's world would be a much better place if he'd stop blabbering long enough for Evan to help him. So, Evan tried a different tack. "Shut up!"

Dinkelman rocked back on his heels as if slapped. His cheeks looked as if he had, turning bright red. He didn't exactly shut up, as his mouth was still open, but no more words were coming out, so that was good.

"George," Evan said, flatly. "I have the names of several people, here in this file, who were involved in the bowling incident – do not interrupt me again – we believe these people are teenagers or adolescents living in Seaview Cove. We need to locate these kids, and you are going to help us."

Dinkelman stared at him, still dumbfounded. Evan couldn't tell whether the man was hearing him or not.

"I want to show you this file that I've put together on the crimes here in Seaview," Evan said, speaking slowly and nodding to Dinkelman as he opened the file on the hood of his Pilot. "I'm very close to solving at least one of these crimes."

Dinkelman seemed to drift toward the open file.

"But I need your help identifying these kids. I believe many of them live right here in Seaview Cove."

Dinkelman peered into the open file as if it were Al Capone's vault. Evan had it open to the page of Paula's report with the names that had been carved into the bowling ball. Dinkelman stared at the list of names for a full minute. Finally, he heaved a great sigh and shook his head.

"I don't understand," he said, head still going from side to side. "I can't comprehend why men in law enforcement feel compelled to let their egos guide them. If you had just come to me with this, from the get-go, so much trouble might have been avoided."

All the hot color was gone from his face and he looked truly shaken. Truly sorrowful, a beaten man, but not broken, destined to carry the weight of the whole world on his sturdy little shoulders until kingdom come if that's what it took. And it probably would.

Crenshaw shot Evan a questioning look behind Dinkelman's back, and Evan shrugged in response.

"George," Evan said, "Do you know any of these names?"

"Of course, I know who they are. They live in my development, don't they?"

Evan saw Crenshaw roll back not just his eyes, but his entire head.

"If you can give us last names for these people," Evan started, "Help us nail down their contact information…"

Dinkelman was shaking his head again, this time not in sorrow but in negation. "This is my development. These are my families."

Evan was about to try again, but before he could, Dinkelman said, "Come with me, let's go have a talk with their parents."

Dinkelman waved them towards his Mercedes, then trudged off in that direction. From the back, with his shoulders slumped, he looked more Shrek-like than ever. Evan nodded for Crenshaw to fall in behind the developer and moved to do the same.

Then his cell buzzed. He checked the number, saw it was Goff, and hit the answer button.

"You want the good news or the bad news, Sheriff?" Goff asked in his good-humored indifference.

Dinkelman had just plopped into the driver's seat. Evan watched him with a twinge of pity for the suspension. Crenshaw was looking back at Evan with a *now-what* question on his face.

Evan had no idea what Goff was up to, as frequently happened, so he said, "Bad news."

Goff chuckled. "Well, that's not going to work. The bad doesn't make any sense without the good."

"So, why give me the option?" Evan asked. He motioned for Crenshaw to get in the car with Dinkelman and held up a finger indicating he'd be just a minute. Crenshaw looked like he'd been asked to babysit. Dinkelman looked like an elementary school teacher who had found a tack on his chair for the forty-third day in a row.

"Folks like having options," Goff said, "Makes them feel like they're in control. You're not busy right now are you?"

"I'm out here at Seaview with Dinkelman," Evan said. "How about you give me the good news, Goff."

"Excellent choice, sir," Goff said, doing a bad imitation of Dinkelman's bad imitation of a British accent. "The good news is, we now know what that piece of metal in our John Doe is, and it's a helpful piece of metal."

"Okay, what is it?" Evan asked, as he knew he was expected to do.

"It's a piece of a C-ration can."

"How do you get a piece of a ration can embedded in your back?"

"Viet Cong used to put grenades in any kind of tin can; ration can, soda can, whatever," Goff said. "Used 'em as booby traps. I only know that because my uncle was there."

"So our guy is a Vietnam vet," Evan said.

"That's what we're thinking."

"So what's the bad news?"

"We don't have his prints yet, so it's gonna be easier to ID this guy, maybe, but not easy," Goff answered.

A friendly *beep beep* came from the Mercedes, drawing his attention. He looked over to see that Crenshaw had swapped sides with Dinkelman and was now sitting behind the wheel, looking entirely too excited. He hung his head out the open window and called, "Hey, Caldwell, c'mon."

Evan walked over and leaned into the window, "Sorry, George, I have an emergent situation. Something has come up… it is critical that we talk to these kids, but this other thing…"

"I got this, Evan," Crenshaw said.

"I'd like to come back tomorrow morning," Evan tried.

"Nonsense," Dinkelman said, "If you have an emergency, tend to it. No offense, but I think Jimmy's capable of talking to some youths."

Crenshaw nodded before Evan had a chance to ask. "I got this," he repeated.

Evan studied the two, then said, "Okay…it's all yours, I guess. But, listen, do not mention the bowling ball. And don't tie this to the Grundy investigation, right? Work it as if you're collecting names for follow-up interviews about the body under the tree."

Crenshaw nodded in agreement. "That way we don't double your murder rate, right George?"

# EIGHTEEN

WHEN EVAN GOT back to the office, it was almost empty. Vi, of course, was in attendance at her rampart, ready to repel all interlopers and seize any infidels. She looked up as Evan walked into the reception area.

"Mr. Caldwell," she intoned with her customary frown. "Sgt. Malnutrition is parked in your office, despite my admonition that he would be better served by waiting for you at his own desk."

"It's okay, Vi," Evan replied as he headed for his closed door. "He called when I was on my way here and asked if he could use my computer. He's got Meyers using his."

"Deputy Meyers has his own computer," Vi said from under fully furled eyebrows.

"IT's got it."

"Oh, never mind," Vi said. "But please advise the man that he defies me at his peril. I do not like him in your office when you aren't present. Moreover, I'm certain that he's eating at your desk."

"I'll take care of it," Evan said, smiling, as he headed past her desk.

As he did, he heard something along the lines of a failing bilge pump from the direction of her feet. He stopped to look and found a cat carrier. Inside, a gray tiger cat sat seething, a white plastic cone around its neck.

"What's this?"

"Why, it's Mr. Fawlty," Vi answered, apparently disappointed that Evan wasn't somehow already on intimate terms with the cat. "He's just come from the vet."

"I thought he got neutered the other day."

"Of course he did," Vi replied patiently. "But we had a small problem of infection. Now, he must wear the cone so he'll leave it alone."

"Huh." Evan started for his door again. "Maybe I should get Plutes neutered again."

He opened his door to find Goff perched in his desk chair in front of the monitor. In front of him were a legal pad with a lot of chicken scratch and a plastic container of what looked to be compost.

"Oh, hey there," Goff said cheerily. He put his spoon down in the cup.

"You bullied your way past Vi?" Evan asked with wonder in his tone.

"How 'bout that? I was on an adrenaline high from the shrapnel thing, but now I'm scared to leave. You can see what she did to the durn cat."

Evan took off his blazer, looked around for somewhere different to put it, and dropped it on one of the visitor's chairs.

"You want a Snack Pack?" Goff asked. "The beautiful one sent me to work with two. Only store-bought thing she ever packs for me, but that's 'cause I like 'em."

"No, thanks, though, Goff."

"Sure thing. Let me un-ass your chair here." Goff stood up, and Evan traded places with him. Goff stood, pudding in hand. "So, here's where we're at. If our man is a Vietnam vet with a shrapnel wound, then he's got a Purple Heart for it, right?"

"I'm not all that familiar with the military," Evan said.

"Well, it's true. Anyhow, there's a registry of Purple Heart recipients, and you can search it all kinds of ways, geography, military action, and so forth."

"Okay, that's promising."

"It's promising, but as you can see there on your screen, there's a haystack of them just in Florida. Narrow it down to the Panhandle, and it's still a crap-ton."

"Okay, so we need a bunch of guys on this, then," Evan said as he stared at the list that said it was seventeen pages long, and could be sorted alphabetically, by branch of service, and several other variables.

"Well, yeah, a whole bunch if we're just gonna focus on the Purple Hearts, but I was thinking."

"Okay." Evan waited for Goff to polish off his pudding and toss the container in the trash can.

"I was thinking the American Legion, the Vietnam Vets of America and so on," Goff said. "They're small and they're local and we might get lucky looking at places like them while we're slogging through this huge list."

Evan nodded. "Yeah, good idea, Goff. Let's—"

Evan was interrupted by the spine-curling buzz of the circa 1980s intercom. He pressed the button.

"Yes, Vi," he said, and he heard a quiet snicker from Goff.

There was a momentary pause, then, "This is Vi."

"Yes, Vi," Evan said, turning away from Goff, who was grinning.

"Chief Beckett from Wewa is on line 2 for you."

"Okay, I'll talk to him. Thanks, Vi."

"My hearing is excellent, Ruben," Vi droned, and Goff lost the grin. They heard the click of the intercom being freed.

Evan looked at Goff. "Do me a favor and stop antagonizing her."

"You're the one that won't let her say 'This is Vi,'" Goff sniffed.

"That's different," Evan said. "Okay, I need to take this call. Put Meyers and Peterson on the local veterans' groups. I'll see if Vi can narrow down our search parameters on this Purple Heart thing."

"Okay, will do," Goff said, and headed out, legal pad in one hand and spoon and extra pudding in the other.

Once he'd opened the door, Evan picked up the blinking line 2.

"Hey, Beckett."

"Hey, Bigtime. You got a minute?"

"Yeah, a couple. What's up?"

"I've been thinking about this Morrow thing."

Beckett had known Tommy Morrow all of the young man's life, and Evan knew that, despite Beckett being the one that had helped him arrest Tommy, he'd been unhappy about it. So had Evan.

"Okay, what's on your mind?" Evan asked him.

"Let's say I cop to taking Tommy's glove off to see if he had an injury from the slide on the murder weapon. How does that help you get this Abernathy woman off your case, and what does it mean for Tommy?"

"Aren't you concerned about what it means for you?"

"Not especially, no. Nobody else wants to be chief of the Wewa police, and it might be bad procedure to take a man's glove off without asking, but it's not exactly a prosecutable offense."

"No, but it could cause a lot of problems for the DA."

"I thought you wanted to slap those on the defense."

"The defense is dying to go to trial," Evan said. "Not to get a plea deal."

There was a moment of silence, then Evan heard Beckett laugh softly.

"If you're not real careful, I might start liking you, Hollywood," Beckett said.

"That's really nice, but are you willing to tell the DA you violated poor Tommy's rights?"

Beckett was quiet for another moment. When he spoke again, his voice was free of humor. "Everybody's violated that boy's rights," he said.

It was true. Evan's late boss, Sheriff Hutchins, had manipulated the simple man into executing him. Now the legal system wanted to try him for first-degree murder as well as conspiracy, since Sheriff Hutchins had paid Tommy at $8500, which Tommy had used to pay his little brother's college tuition.

Tommy Morrow, who had the cognitive and emotional function of a preadolescent, had been convinced that what he was being asked to do was not only right, but noble. Now he sat in the county jail, reading comic books and hoping for visitors. Evan managed to get there once a month or so.

"I don't disagree, Beckett," Evan said. "Each of us knows where the other stands."

"Well, talk to the DA," Beckett said. "I'll stand by whatever you tell him."

"Careful, Beckett, I might start taking a liking to you, too."

"Well, hell, maybe we can go out dancing sometime," replied Beckett, who was as heterosexual as anyone Evan had ever met.

Evan smiled. "I'm really not the go-out-dancing type," he said.

"But, you're Cuban, man."

Evan didn't balk at the stereotyping. He suspected it wasn't sincere.

"The couple that adopted me were Scottish and English. I'm really only Cuban when I drink."

"Huh. Well, give me a shout next time you're having a cocktail."

Beckett hung up, and Evan smiled into the phone.

"I might actually do that," he said to the dead line, then hung up the phone.

A couple hours later, Evan was on his way to Seaview Cove. Crenshaw had called to say that Dinkelman had helped him round up the kids who'd carved their names into Grundy's bowling ball, and once at least one parent for each child was in attendance, Crenshaw had talked to the kids as a group. They were all still there, gathered in the partially-finished clubhouse across the access road from Grundy's backyard. Evan needed out of the office, so he opted to drive over there rather than have Crenshaw relay the results over the phone.

Crenshaw was waiting outside the clubhouse's double doors, drinking a Slurpee, when Evan pulled up.

"Hey, Boss," Crenshaw said as Evan approached.

"Hey," Evan answered, lighting a cigarette. He glanced across the street at the lot where the kids had wrecked all of Dinkelman's precious evidence. "So, what's up?"

"Well, you can go in there and talk to the kids and the parents yourself, but I don't think you need to. They all seem like halfway decent kids. Bored, maybe, entitled for sure, but not bad like some other kids we've seen on the job."

"What's the upshot?" Evan asked.

"They all say the same thing, and they all stick to the same details. They didn't have anything to do with any landscaping, and they didn't see anybody around the night before the body was discovered. They all copped to underage drinking in some of the empty houses, and they all say they found the ball in the lot across the street on Saturday night. They bowled with their empties and left a mess and the ball, but that's it."

Evan smoked and thought for a moment. "You feel pretty good about it?" he asked Crenshaw finally.

Crenshaw was in the middle of a rattling draw on his Slurpee. Evan waited.

"Yeah, boss, I do," Crenshaw said.

Evan nodded and turned to look behind him at the back of Grundy's house.

"Those kids would freak if they knew what you were thinking," Crenshaw said.

"What do you think I'm thinking?" Evan asked.

"That somebody caved Grundy's head in with his own bowling ball and dumped it over here, and those kids had their hands all over it half the night." Crenshaw shrugged. "Which, when I was fifteen or so, would have creeped me way out."

Evan nodded, his eyes narrowing against the smoke from his cigarette as he looked at Grundy's place.

"That's what we're thinking, right?" Crenshaw asked.

Evan ground out his cigarette with his toes, then picked up the butt. "Something like that."

Evan tried to make it a policy not to check his cell phone or even get on his cell once he was on the boat. He parked in one of the open spaces behind the Dockside Grill, pulled out his phone, and checked for new messages, then checked his email. He answered two that required it and deleted the rest, then grabbed the organic milk he'd gotten at The Pig and got out of the car.

The steps down to the dock were bookended by the Dockside Grill's covered patio on the left and a firepit and seating area on the right. There were a few people on the patio, and an elderly woman reading a paperback by the unlit firepit, but Evan didn't know any of them and was relieved he didn't have to say hello to anyone.

His hard-soled shoes thumped sharply against the wood planks of the dock. His slip was a T-slip at the end of the south pier, and when he turned left he saw Plutes sitting across from the fish cleaning station on the corner of their pier. He did that a lot; sat there watching and waiting for whatever. When they'd first moved onto the boat, three months after Hannah's accident, Evan had assumed he was waiting for Hannah to come home. He'd been her cat, although she'd only brought the thing home a couple of weeks before she couldn't come home anymore.

In any event, he wasn't waiting for Evan, because as soon as he saw Evan, he always turned and walked away.

Except for today. Today, he sat there like a gargoyle, eyes mere slits, as he watched Evan approach.

"How's it going?" Evan asked with disinterest as he passed the cat and turned onto their pier.

He looked toward his slip and saw that Sarah was leaning against the power hookup pole for his slip. She was batting at her phone with her thumbs. Playing a game or texting at the speed of light, Evan assumed. He texted with one finger and was flipping proud of it.

Something caught his eye, and he looked down to see Plutes keeping pace with him, with that weird little cat trot that cats who are trotting do. Maybe he'd learned to read milk cartons.

Sarah looked up as Evan approached, and smiled at him, then noticed Plutes and smiled wider. She was smart enough not to mention his escort.

"Hey," she said, in her squeaky-raspy voice. She tucked her phone into the back pocket of her modestly mid-thigh cut-offs.

"Hey."

"I was taking out the trash when you pulled in, so I thought I'd wait for you," she said.

"Do you need something?" Evan asked as he stopped in front of her.

"Nah, I just wanted to say 'hey,'" she said, shrugging. "I did kinda want to talk to you about something, though. Ask for your help with something."

Evan looked at her for a moment. "Are you in trouble?"

"No, nothing like that," she said quickly. "More like a favor?"

Evan watched as Plutes landed in the aft cockpit with a thud and nimbly climbed the steps up to the sundeck.

"Well, come on up," he said. "Let me put this milk away."

"Okay."

She kicked off her flip-flops, followed him up the dock boarding steps, and took a seat at the rattan table. She'd been aboard several times, but never past the sundeck. Given what he'd found out about Abby Abernathy's defense strategy, Evan was grateful for that.

"You want something to drink?" Evan asked as he slipped off his shoes by the door.

"No, thanks." Plutes jumped into her lap and she started scratching behind his ears. Plutes had never been in Evan's lap, not that he'd ever been invited to strew his black fur all over Evan's pants, but Evan always found himself a little offended that the cat was so fond of her.

"I'll be right back," he said, opening the French door. He left it open, jogged down the four steps into the salon. He noticed the African violet was unmolested as he crossed the salon, stepped down into the galley, and put the milk in the residential-sized stainless fridge. He grabbed a bottle of water for himself, then decided to grab one for her, too, and went back out to the sundeck.

The idiot was actually on his back on the girl's lap, feet up in the air like a dead and bloated possum. Evan sighed, handed her the water, and sat down across the table from her,

"Thanks," Sarah said as she twisted off the cap.

"So, what's up?"

"Um, well, you know how I got my GED when I was sixteen and stuff, but I never took my SATs. I was thinking maybe I should."

"Did you check to see if Gulf State requires SATs? Because they probably don't."

"No, they don't." She took a small drink of her water. "But I was thinking it wouldn't hurt to apply to a few other places. Maybe even Florida State." She shrugged one bony shoulder and gave him a nervous smile. "I mean, maybe there's a scholarship for the kids of felons or meth heads or whatever."

"In Florida? Probably," he said and tried to give her a reassuring smile.

"Can't hurt to try, right?"

"Right." Evan took a swallow of the water. It was cold and clean and sweet and felt tremendous going down his throat.

"Well, so anyway, the thing is, I never took any math higher than Algebra I and I'm having trouble with the math in this SAT practice book I got at the library."

"You want to know if I can help you with math?" Evan asked, surprised.

"Well, yeah." She broke his gaze, looked down at the cat as she rubbed his stomach.

"I guess I can do that," Evan said. "My math's pretty good."

"Man, thanks," she said, her smile wide. "It would make me feel good to do okay with this book anyway, but how cool would it be if I got in somewhere good, right? Even if I couldn't afford to go."

Evan suddenly wished he had thousands of dollars sitting in a 401k, but he'd already drained that, with heavy penalties.

"That would be cool," he agreed.

"Where did you go?"

"University of Miami. I wanted to go out of state, but my adoptive parents were in their fifties when they took me in, and my adoptive father passed away my senior year of high school, so I thought I should stay close. She ended up passing away my junior year of college."

"Aw." Sarah looked genuinely saddened by this. "Do you have any other family?"

Evan took another drink before he answered. "No. The Caldwells had a daughter that died when she was twenty. Leukemia, long before I met them. They didn't have any other family that I know of."

Sarah stared at him a moment. "Well, I've got a lot of relatives, but I wouldn't really call any of them family. Isn't any one of 'em straight."

Evan nodded, and they sat in silence for a moment. She scratched the fat black fool behind the ears and he considered her for a minute.

"Listen," he said finally. "I'm happy to tutor you, help you with your math, whatever, when I have time. But, we're probably gonna have to do that up at the Grill or in the library or something."

"Okay. Why?" Her perfectly-arched black brows curled together.

"There's somebody going around trying to dig up some dirt on me," Evan answered. "It's a long story; it's got to do with a trial coming up. But they've had somebody following me around. They even have pictures of you and me on the runabout. They're trying to make some kind of thing about it."

"You mean like we're going out or something?" she asked, seeming incredulous.

"Something like that, yeah." He felt like maybe he should apologize to her for that.

"That's so lame," she said indignantly. "People of different genders can have perfectly innocent relationships."

He tried not to cringe at the word 'relationship.' It was a lifelong problem, almost a tic, but he managed to

control it in this instance. "This isn't a perfectly innocent world."

"I mean, you're really handsome and everything, but
you're not my vibe, you know? I go for skinny nerds.
Well, not right now, but I would."

Evan couldn't help thinking of Danny. Danny would
be good enough for her, if he wasn't twenty-six.

"I'm sorry," he said. He pulled out his cigarettes and
lit one.

"Geez, people suck," she said. "I mean, if anything,
you're more like a father figure."

Evan huffed out a laugh, the origin of which was
terror more than humor.

"You're old enough to be my dad, you know."

Evan felt that tic coming on. "I'm old enough to be
a lot of people's dads, but there are many good reasons
I'm not."

He saw that this had been received like a pushback,
saw it in the quick blink and the swallow. He hadn't
meant it to hurt, he'd just meant it to deflect.

"If I was your dad, though, I'd be pretty damn proud
of it."

"Why?"

Evan took a long drag of his cigarette and blew the
smoke out away from her before he answered. "Because
you were born into a situation that usually creates addicts,
teenaged parents, abusers, depressives, and felons, and
you came out of it a decent and smart and caring person."

It took her a minute to answer. He watched her stare at him while she thought.

"So did you," she said simply.

It was Evan's turn to blink, but in his case, it was due to surprise. He and Sarah were so different. She was warm, he was cold. She reached out, he retreated. She took strength in her faith; he didn't know if he'd ever had any. It had never occurred to him how much they actually had in common.

After a minute he realized he'd been staring at her too long.

"Interesting observation," he said quietly.

"The obvious, you mean?" she asked dryly.

"Don't be a jerk."

# NINETEEN

EVAN SPENT MOST of the next morning reading over the results of the latest complaint and arrest reports. Then he leafed through the notes his deputies had filed regarding the canvassing of Grundy's neighborhood. Nothing new had come in on that front. Many of the local kids had long ago decided that the last house on the block was the neighborhood's haunted house.

According to the threadbare plot of the local lore, an elderly couple had lived in that house before "Dr. Grumpy," as they called him, and somehow their bodies ended up under the wheelchair ramp, which was the real reason he never removed it. The how's and why's of this story didn't follow any traceable grown-up logic and made no difference whatsoever to the kids telling it. However, after his finds in the doll room, Evan had a difficult time discounting the story out of hand. He made a note to look into who had owned the property before Grundy.

That would have to wait. He had put a plan in motion during morning muster, calling out Deputy Holland and acknowledging his significant contributions to the Grundy case, first by pointing Evan to the Cracker Bowl, and then by identifying Grundy's bowling ball. His fellow deputies had chided Holland with good-natured jibes, which he bore with much less irritation than he typically expressed.

Evan went on to say that he and Holland would be going back to Grundy's house this afternoon to do a second survey of the crime scene. This garnered a raised eyebrow from Goff, who then scratched names off his duty roster, then rearranged the assignments. Paula had finished processing the house itself. She was now cataloging and examining Grundy's trophies at her lab. Evan felt that they might be able to get a better sense of the scene by walking the house without its eerie inanimate occupants to distract them.

"As to the Grundy house, and the items that Paula has collected," Evan said, addressing the disgruntled murmuring the subject elicited from his deputies, "We are going to continue to keep that under wraps for the time being."

This brought more groans and sounds of disapproval.

"I will give you a brief synopsis. He kept trophies of a very disturbing nature. So far, the items we've recovered suggest no crime above a level of a misdemeanor, but they would be very upsetting to family or friends of those he performed autopsies on. It is a scandal that would hurt a lot of people. Speculation would be even worse than the truth, but the truth is bad enough."

Meyers spoke up, lending his support, "I know it sucks to be on the outside of a secret. This time, though, trust me, guys, you don't want to know."

Evan said, "In the short time I've been with you, I have found you to be law enforcement personnel of the finest caliber, and you constantly exceed my expectations. This is not an issue of trust. I'm doing my best to keep you out of a situation you don't want to be in. This way, you won't have to keep secrets from your families, but you won't have to tell them something you would never want them to hear."

The explanation didn't fully satisfy his troops. He'd been under no illusion that it would, but he could feel their attitudes soften. It would be enough for now.

Only Evan, Meyers, Goff, Paula and Danny had seen the doll room that night. Evan assumed that Sgt. Peters had taken a peek at the room he had been assigned to guard, though he hadn't admitted it and Evan hadn't asked him. The man's silent support of Evan's position on the matter suggested more knowledge of the subject than he would have gathered if he had just waited in the hall as instructed.

Danny was not, technically, under Evan's command, but had agreed not to discuss the subject of the dolls with anyone who wasn't already privy to the information. Beyond these, no one else knew what they had found in Grundy's back bedroom. Evan felt he needed to add one more deputy to the inner circle.

He believed, and hoped, that if he could break the glacier between himself and Holland, he might someday have a chance at fitting into his community. He had never felt a strong drive to pursue acceptance or high status, but being an outsider made him the target of any nearby spotlight. Being constantly reminded that he wasn't one of them was an annoyance he could do without.

Also, he figured Paula might be able to use an assistant to help her process all those dolls.

Now, as the lunch hour waned, and the various smells from the station's microwave dissipated, Evan heard a knock on his open door. He looked up from the pile of reports on his desk to see Goff, Meyers and Holland lined up at his threshold. This exceeded Vi's threshold of two people in her sphere at any given time.

"Heading down to the VFW," Goff said, "Meyers has got his dues up to date, so he's going with."

"Hey, I'm a vet," Holland said. "Why do you guys get to go to a bar, while I'm stuck with the boss man at a murder house?"

"That was your idea, remember?" Evan said. "Besides Holland, I took you to the bar last time."

"What do you mean, my idea?"

"You asked to see what was in the boxes," Evan said, leaning back in his chair, "Your wish is being granted. You seem to know more about Grundy than anyone else I've got. I figure that is some pretty important knowledge right now."

Holland eyed him suspiciously.

"I'm serious," Evan said. "This guy is an enigma. You've been the only one to come up with any useful information about him so far, and we need that to figure out what was going on with him. I'm not opening those Grundy boxes for anyone else, but I think there's a chance you'll see something the rest of us might miss."

"You know, after what you said this morning, maybe I'm okay not knowing," Holland said, shifting his eyes to the side to check Goff's response.

There was none.

"Look, Holland," Evan said. "I need you with me out at the Grundy house today, doing a walkthrough. I have no qualms about showing you the evidence that we took out of there if you want to see it, but I'm leaving that up to you."

Holland still looked suspicious, but he was nodding. The grin he wore suggested to Evan that he had taken the offer as a challenge. "Sure," he said, "I'll take a peek."

"Well, we're gonna head on out," Goff said. "Those fellers down there said if we got there before eleven, we might still get some biscuits and gravy."

Before he turned to go, he dropped a hand on Holland's shoulder. "Anybody ever tell you be careful what you wish for?"

Evan drove so Holland could flip through the inch-thick folder of photos from Grundy's house. He had not yet gotten to the photos of the doll room when Evan turned in to Grundy's neighborhood.

"What is it I'm supposed to be looking for, here?" Holland asked.

"If I knew that, I wouldn't need you along, right?" Evan said.

"No, you'd probably still need me."

"I didn't know to ask you about the ball," Evan said. "I'm wondering what else I don't know to ask you about."

"Look, it's not like we were buddies," Holland said, flopping the folder closed. "I've never been to his house. We didn't hang out after work. I just knew about Cracker Bowl because I see him there on Fridays, when I go."

Evan pulled to the curb outside the only yellow-tape festooned wheelchair ramp on the last street to the left. "Ever bowl a frame with him?"

"Sure, once or twice," Holland said dismissively. "Everybody did. Teams were always getting switched up. That's how I knew about the ball."

The two men exited the Pilot, slipped under the tape and headed around back to the back deck.

"Was he any good?" Evan asked, his loafers crunching on the yellowed grass.

Holland chuckled, "Depended on how deep in his cups he was."

"Was he ever too sober to bowl straight?" Evan asked, and that almost surprised a laugh out of Holland.

He turned his head to the side, so Evan wouldn't see the smile, composed himself, then responded, "He had a sweet spot. Too many gin and tonics and his arm would go all linguini. Gutter ball more often than not. Too few, and he'd get a seven or eight at best. He'd say his joints were squeaking and needed more lube."

Evan noticed that the man actually seemed at ease for the first time in memory.

"But get him right around a 2.0 blood alcohol level and he'd strike more often than spare."

Evan smiled. It seemed like the right response, but when he turned to Holland to comment, he realized it must not have been. The deputy was as stony-faced as ever. Evan kept his comment to himself.

They entered through the slider, as they had done the night they'd found Grundy.

The decomp odor was still thick, thick enough that Evan thought he could actually feel it on his exposed skin, but it wasn't as sharp as it had been. The lights were out, and the curtains pulled, making the empty house feel stuffy and claustrophobic.

A spider had moved into the dining area, spinning its trap from the light above the table to the archway leading to the hall. Maybe it hoped the smell would attract its dinner. The house had been tidily kept when they found it, but after more than a week unattended, dust and additional webs had begun asserting themselves. This in addition to fingerprint dust on most visible surfaces. Nothing interesting had come of that.

"The laundry room, kitchen and dining room are as we found them," Evan explained, "Except for the print dust. Paula didn't identify anything in here that seemed out of place."

"Looks like an old drunk's kitchen," Holland said. "Okay, maybe cleaner than I expected. Does that help?"

"No," Evan said, evenly, "Goff and Meyers got that sorted out shortly after they arrived."

Holland was facing into the house with Evan behind and to his right. He put his hands on his gun belt, looked at the floor, then turned to face Evan. "I know what you're up to, Caldwell," he said, nodding his head and grinning cynically. "You're trying to play me."

"I'm not playing you, Holland, I'm trying to work with you."

Holland appraised him for a moment, made a sucking sound through his teeth, then eventually said, "You know, there was a reason everybody liked Hutch. Say whatever you want about how he ended it and I won't argue, but he was good people and he belonged here."

Evan thought he might be able to challenge him on the concept of *good people*, but the word *belong* stuck in his mind and he couldn't quite get around it before Holland continued.

"We don't need strangers coming in from God knows where to solve our problems, set us straight, teach us how to do what we've been doing for God knows how long before you showed up."

Evan waited for him to finish.

"Especially someone who's got worse problems than we do. Someone who sees being here as some sort of penance...or someone trying to redeem himself by fixing us, since his own life went way past fixing. I find it insulting."

That last bit was almost physical. Evan felt it in his chest, but he knew it didn't show. He'd had a flawless poker face since he was seven years old and in his fourth foster home.

"I would too," Evan said after a moment. "You let me know if someone like that shows up. We'll rustle up a posse and run the bastard out of town."

Holland's jaw clenched; the muscles at its corners protruded. He stood two inches taller than Evan, with a barrel chest and a neck thicker than his head. But, Evan had grown up scrapping with boys that always seemed to be at least two inches taller and twenty pounds heavier and didn't feel any more intimidated by Holland than he had by any of those other foster kids.

"If you have something against me, Holland," Evan unclipped his holster and set it on Grundy's table, "if there is something you want to say to me," he laid his badge and Sheriff's credentials beside his weapon. "I'd appreciate it if you would just speak your mind." He stepped away from the table. "Man to man."

"Oh, good golly," Holland scoffed. "You want to duke it out in a dead guy's kitchen? What's wrong with you, man?"

"I'm not fighting you," Evan said. "I'm giving you the opportunity to say what you want to say; get it out in the open as a peer, like a grown-up."

"I think I've said all I'm going to, Caldwell," Holland said, then changed his mind. "We all know the only reason you got the big chair is so your commissioner pal can pull your strings. He must have something on you." Evan didn't try to interrupt, but Holland held up a hand as if he had. "But more than that, we all know about you and your wife. You got some kind of emotional knot going on with that, guilt, anger, whatever, and I guess I can't fault you for that. But then you ride into town, fresh off a thing like that and start preaching at us…" He made the sucking sound through his teeth again, as he refocused.

Evan waited.

Holland continued, "Maybe Hutch was hard on her sometimes, but she never left him, never went running around behind his back. So, what's that tell you, huh? You're no Hutch, that's what I'm saying, I didn't think much of you when you were a lieutenant, and I think even less of you now. Sitting in that office like you belong. You're no Hutch."

The foster homes had also proved to be excellent training in how to deflect verbal abuse. Holland's attacks on Evan's marriage were sharp blows on open wounds, and they cut deeply, mainly because they carried an element of truth. But the same could have been said of all the ridicule he had endured as a foster child, lines about how even his mother didn't want him around.

When he had been young, these attacks had almost always turned physical, with either he or his taunter leaving blood on the ground. But, Evan was smart and had learned quickly that people who brutalize others with their words for the mere pleasure of it were cowards and did not merit a response. Or, just as often, the attacker was suffering their own pain and felt some measure of relief by sharing the experience. Either way, allowing even the most painful of words to elicit a violent response seldom worked out in anyone's favor.

On the other hand, allowing disrespect with impunity had negative consequences, as well,

"You get away with that, once," Evan said quietly. "Talking about my marriage, my wife, is way out of bounds, and you know it, but I'm giving you a pass this time because I asked what was on your mind, and I wanted an honest answer. But, do not mention her again unless you're asking after her wellbeing. Anything else, and I will be fired and you will be on disability. It's essential for you to understand how sincere I am when I say this."

Holland didn't want to give anything, but Evan waited. Eventually, the deputy allowed a single, grudging nod.

"How long did you work for Hutch?" Evan asked.

Holland jerked his head back. "Work for him? Man, I knew him my whole life. My mom still lives next door to his empty house. Marlene can't even find a buyer for it so she can move out of her daughter's house and get her own little place."

Evan almost, automatically, asked Holland if, in all the years he'd lived next door, he'd never heard Marlene Hutchins being beaten. But then he realized that maybe he had, maybe as a child, and either never admitted it or was never able to do anything about it. Maybe that's where all this animosity really came from. Evan sighed.

"I'm not here to set all your backwoods yokels straight. I'm just here because it's the best I can do for my wife right now. Me being here pisses you off? That doesn't even register anywhere on my list of priorities. At all."

Holland did not respond, but Evan had his attention, and he could tell the deputy was hearing him, at least on some level.

Evan pressed on, "I'm not talking to you as a boss, Holland. I'm talking man to man; I have a job to do. You've got a job to do. We don't have to hang out after hours or join a knitting circle. We don't even have to like each other, but it'd make both our lives much easier if you could drop the animosity, or at least keep it to yourself."

"If I wanted an easy life, I'd move to Cocoa Beach," Holland said, but it was more of an obligatory swipe. His color had gone down and the anger in his voice was barely detectable now. "I've said what I had to say, Caldwell. And I'd say it all the same if you asked again, but I don't think you're gonna."

Evan confirmed this with a nod.

"You know what I think of you," Holland said, "By now, everybody else does too. It ain't changing and I didn't make a secret of it, but sure, I can keep it to myself. At least on the job. I can do that for you."

Evan wondered if he expected gratitude.

"I got one other thing you need to hear," Holland said. "'A life is not defined by its final act.' I read that in a book about suicide. I think it's pretty important for you to keep in mind; maybe temper your sermons a bit."

It took Evan a breath or two to realize the deputy had been talking about Hutch, not Hannah. Evan had been thinking of his wife's final act, a romantic tryst on her lover's boat. Holland was right, it did not define her, but that comment hit Evan harder than any of the man's intentional attacks. Her final act did not define her, but Evan felt that somehow it defined him.

"Yeah," Holland said, not gloating but satisfied. "That got through to you. He was a good man, Caldwell; you need to remember that. And you're not him."

"No," Evan said, "No, I'm not. I've never raised my hand to a woman."

A silence passed between them, the tectonic plates of each other's view of the other settling back into place, not far from where they had started.

Chatter on Holland's police radio brought them both back to the moment. Holland checked his radio, determined the traffic didn't involve them, then said, "It stinks in here. Let's do whatever the hell we came here to do and get out."

# TWENTY

OVER THE NEXT thirty minutes or so, Evan and Holland toured Grundy's house, examining the rooms and consulting the stack of photos anywhere the room's appearance had been altered after its discovery by evidence collection or other investigative activities. Both did so with complete emotional detachment, almost robotically.

At first, Holland's comments were as useful as his initial assessment of Grundy's kitchen, but as they progressed through the rooms, he seemed to give his answers a bit more thought. He noted the absence of any clothes other than Grundy's indicating that the man had no houseguests when he was killed. He confirmed this assumption by a quick perusal through the man's medicine cabinets and toiletries. He observed, based on the food in the refrigerator and the dishes in the sink, that it was highly unlikely that Grundy had had company that day.

The conclusion he drew was that whoever killed Grundy had come from outside the home to do so. The locked front door and open slider in back suggested to Holland that the killer had probably knocked on the slider door then clubbed the doctor when he answered. Of course, this meant Grandy probably knew his attacker, or at least that the attacker didn't seem threatening, since Grundy would have been able to clearly see who was standing at the sliding glass door.

Evan let Holland proceed through these logical warm-ups before directing his attention to anything that hadn't been obvious to him within minutes of entering. He asked Holland if Grundy's odd choice of shirts meant anything, showing him the photo of the red and yellow polyester polo. Holland dismissed that as normal; it was his lucky shirt he'd always wear when he went bowling.

There had been speculation that robbery might have been a motive, though that was unlikely. Grundy had a large class ring he usually wore when not performing autopsies, but it was not on his finger when he was found. Holland put this to rest, stating that he never wore the ring when bowling, for obvious reasons.

He studied the photos of Grundy's body slumped against the laundry room wall, one foot in the closet, one foot under him, the contents of his reusable Piggly Wiggly shopping tote scattered on and around him, and gave a sad chuckle, "Geez. He was a character," Holland mused, finally opening up a bit. "A lot of the guys buy these fancy leather satchels for their balls. Grundy always called those things 'purses.' He was forever joking about guys carrying their balls in a purse. I guess he thought carrying his ball in a Piggly Wiggly tote was more manly."

Evan looked at him for a moment, then looked down at the photo of the bag. "You don't say. I'm not sure I follow that logic though."

"No, I don't guess you would," Holland replied. He sounded annoyed that it was Evan he was talking to. "I don't know, Caldwell, I don't know what you were hoping I'd see out here. It's Grundy. It's Grundy's house. No great revelations. No big secrets."

"Photos of that empty guest room are in the last flap of that folder."

Holland rolled his eyes, then proceeded to flip through the folder.

Evan waited while Holland looked at the first few photos, very slowly. The deputy struggled mightily to appear unfazed by the experience. It was a valiant effort, but ultimately unsuccessful. He was just a shade too pale, and his eyes just a tick too wide, when he looked up again.

"Any of that mean anything to you?" Evan asked.

Holland didn't say anything, just slowly walked past Evan, dropping the folder of photos on the kitchen counter, and walked out the laundry room to the back deck.

Evan calmly retrieved the folder, along with his badge and gun, before following Holland out. The deputy turned to look at him.

"You honestly think I would have gone in there with you if I'd known anything about that?" Holland asked.

He walked around to the front of the house, where they had parked. As Evan rounded the garage, he heard Holland say, "Should have taken two cars."

· ● ✳ ● ·

They drove in silence out of Grundy's neighborhood. As they pulled back onto the main drag, Evan's phone rang, and he answered it.

"Hey, Sheriff, it's Meyers." The deputy was excited, a welcome relief to his current company.

"Go ahead, Meyers," Evan said. "What have you got?"

"I think we've identified our John DOA," Meyers said. "The old-timers do a good job keeping tabs on each other, knowing who's where and what's what."

"Sure," Evan said. "By old-timers, you mean the Vietnam vets?"

"Oh, well, yeah," Meyers hesitated, "No disrespect, though."

"Okay," Evan said. "So, what did you learn?"

"A few of those guys were awarded a Purple Heart, and most will tell you the story if you buy them a beer, right?"

"Sure," Evan said.

"There was a guy, Daniel Miner, who got hit by one of those Viet Cong tin can grenades, just like we're looking for. He used to be down there once or twice a month on Monday nights for bingo or Wednesdays for hamburger night," Meyers said. "But a while back he stopped showing up. A couple of the guys went to look in on him, but the family gave them the cold shoulder, said he had passed away and they didn't want to talk about it."

"Really?" Evan said, sitting up a little bit straighter. "Did you get any more details on Daniel Miner's injury?"

"Yes sir," Meyers said. "This has got to be our guy. He told the guys that he had part of a ration can stuck by his spine."

"Okay, yeah," Evan said, looking over at Holland to include him in the conversation, "That sounds like our guy. We'll subpoena Mr. Miner's medical records for confirmation in the morning. Good work, Meyers."

"Thank you, sir. Goff's idea, though."

"Have you started trying to track down Miner's last address?"

"Sure, we tried. No driver's license, but Goff put a call in to city records. The VFW guys said he lived in town – but records has closed for the evening. We'll get his address first thing in the morning."

Evan checked the dashboard clock and realized it was after five already.

Meyers continued, "Goff and I started going through the list Dinkelman provided, all the construction workers and landscape people he had on payroll in the twelve to eighteen months ago timeframe," he said, "Just looking for anyone with the last name Miner. No luck so far, but it's a pretty big stack of names."

"Okay, good plan, "Evan said, "But wrap it up; we can hit that again in the morning."

"Okay, sounds good," Meyers said. "I'll see you then."

Holland was happier than Evan had ever seen him when he slid out of Evan's car and shut the door behind him. Evan checked in with Vi, checked back out, and headed home.

The hallway to Hannah's room was as hushed as usual, but not empty. As Evan made his way toward Hannah's room, a backpack slung over his right shoulder, he saw Hannah's doctor talking to the nurses at the nurse's station. Dr. Richman saw him, too, and waited until Evan was almost there before meeting him partway.

Evan stopped. Plutes growled. Richman looked at the backpack, looked back at Evan and sighed.

"Mr. Caldwell, what is that?"

"Well, it's not her cat," Evan replied quietly.

The doctor sighed again. Evan liked Richman. In his Dockers and his plaid button-down shirts, he was as accessible and non-threatening a doctor as he should be. The wire-rimmed glasses and wispy blond hair helped.

"Mr. Caldwell, I realize that you will probably try to push me off again, and I understand, but it is absolutely imperative that we talk about your situation."

"You mean *her* situation?" Evan asked, not unkindly.

"No, I mean yours, Evan," Richman answered. "She has no knowledge of her situation. Her situation does not affect her at all."

Evan turned to look at an oil painting of a ship on a placid sea. He didn't feel like a ship on a placid sea.

"Evan, I know this facility will be more than happy to continue taking your money, as long as you're able to keep giving them the money your insurance company won't. But *my* only reason for letting this continue this long was to give you closure. However, as I told you six months ago, closure that doesn't lead to moving forward isn't closure at all."

Evan looked back at the doctor as Plutes grumbled and shifted around.

"I hear you," he said simply.

"You always tell me that, but it doesn't mean much."

Evan nodded, looked at his shoes a moment, then looked back up. "I'm going to take her cat in there for a bit."

Richman gave him a sympathetic look that Evan knew to be sincere and without empty pity. "She's not going to respond to her cat, Evan."

"I know that," Evan said. "It's not for her; it's for the cat. I thought he might want to say goodbye."

Richman looked at him a moment, then nodded. "Call me or leave me a message when you want to discuss this further."

Evan nodded, then continued on to Hannah's room.

The room seemed warmer than usual, and Evan almost wanted to prop open the door, but he let it whoosh closed behind him. The room was exactly as it had been the night before. So was Hannah.

Evan sighed, walked around the bed, and then put the backpack down on the lavender blanket. Plutes growled as Evan put his hands under his shoulders and lifted him out of the backpack.

"Shut up," Evan said without any real enthusiasm.

Evan plopped the cat down on the bed, then he sat down in the little upholstered chair. Plutes sniffed at the backpack, then sniffed at the blanket. He took a few steps toward Hannah's face, stepping over the pale arm that lay still as stone.

The cat glanced at Hannah, then jumped over the rail and onto the little nightstand, then down to the floor.

"What's wrong with you?" Evan hissed at the cat. "It's her. Sit with her a minute."

Plutes looked at him, then walked away. Evan watched him nose around the small room. He didn't understand how cats' minds worked. The fatass had walked around the marina for months, looking for her, Evan had assumed. Now he acted like she wasn't in the room.

Evan was ranting about that in his head as he watched Plutes stop to give his leg a tongue lashing. After a moment, it popped into Evan's head to wonder how long Hannah had known the cat. She'd brought him home about two weeks before her accident, brought her boyfriend's cat into *their* home but he had no idea how long Shayne had had the cat. For the first time, it occurred to him that it was possible the cat had known Evan longer than he'd known Hannah.

Plutes looked up at him like he'd heard him talking, then gave his leg one more long lick before walking toward Evan's chair. He sat down about a foot away, looked up at Evan, and gave him one of his inscrutable, slow blinks.

When Evan blinked back, his vision blurred, and one lone tear slid down to his chin.

# TWENTY-ONE

DANIEL MINER'S HOME was a modest 1950s bungalow in a neighborhood of modest 1950s bungalows just west of downtown. Evan had looked at this neighborhood before he'd bought the boat; the homes there no longer carried modest, 1950s prices.

Goff sat beside Evan, drinking coffee from his favorite gas station. Evan, as usual, had brought his *café con leche* from home. He hoped someone would pop an air bubble into one of his veins if he was ever left with no choice other than gas station coffee, but he couldn't think of anyone who cared about him that much.

On Goff's lap was a slim file folder compiled by Vi, with the help of Danny, Toby Ebersole, and several deputies. Fifteen minutes earlier, Crenshaw and Meyers, who sat in separate cars in separate driveways, had notified

Goff that Brian Draper, stepson of Daniel Miner, had just gotten home from his second job.

Vi had managed to find a decent amount of information via internet and telephone calls to various agencies. Goff and the deputies had found their own decent amount by observation.

Goff looked toward Crenshaw, who sat in a neighbor's driveway in a brown minivan with stick figure people all over the back window, then quickly returned his gaze to the front. Ahead, Evan saw the house where Meyers waited in a Red Civic that actually belonged to the neighbor, who had given him the keys and then gone inside to watch Hulu. One block over, Peters and Holland waited in a minivan across the street from Miner's backyard.

Evan pulled into the driveway of Miner's bungalow, parking behind a blue late-model Kia and an older, maroon Saturn. He and Goff got out, Goff leaving his coffee and taking the file.

The house was neat enough, but Evan could see that it needed pressure washing in some places and painting in others, and most of the two flowerbeds were being overrun with weeds. The lawn was mowed, but it didn't look like anyone was keeping things up.

Evan knocked on the door. To his right, underneath what looked like a bedroom window, an HVAC unit's fan hummed. After a moment, a middle-aged African American woman opened the door. Her hair was pinned back, and a rhinestone butterfly twinkled in the sunlight. She wore light pink scrubs covered with different-colored stars.

"May I help you?" she asked, her voice warm and smooth.

"Yes, ma'am," Evan answered. "We're here to see Brian Draper."

She looked over her shoulder for just a second, then back at Evan. Her gaze swept over Goff, resplendent in his khaki-colored uniform and the utility belt that weighed half as much as he did. Then she blinked a couple of times at Evan.

"Aren't you the new sheriff?" She wasn't nervous or uncomfortable, just curious.

Evan smiled at her politely. "Yes, ma'am. May I ask who you are?"

"I'm Carol Howard. I'm the home health care nurse," she answered. "Come in."

She opened the door wider and stepped back so that Evan and Goff could enter. They were in a small living room, with light blue couches decorated with needlepoint and cross-stitched pillows. On the walls were a number of cheap oil paintings, and a lot of photos of an older man and woman, sometimes together, sometimes not.

Evan pointed at a picture of the elderly man, who was wearing a khaki vest and holding up what looked like a bass. Evan wasn't sure; he only knew saltwater fish. He gestured at the picture. "Is this Mr. Miner? Daniel Miner?"

"Yes, that's him," she answered.

"Do you know Mr. Miner?"

"Mr. Miner's passed," Carol answered. She looked a little confused. "Over a year ago, I think."

"Did you know him?" Evan asked her casually.

"No. No, I've only been working here for about seven months," she answered.

"I see."

"I care for *Mrs.* Miner," she added.

"Is she ill?" Evan asked.

"I'm not permitted to say," she answered.

"I'm sorry. Can I ask what kind of nursing you do?"

"I work with Alzheimer's patients, mostly," she said after a slight hesitation.

"Thank you," Evan said.

They all looked at each for a moment that lasted long enough to get awkward.

"Mr. Draper was in the shower," the nurse said finally. "Do you want me to see if he's out?"

"Yes, thank you," Evan said, trying to reassure her with a smile. "I'd appreciate it, though, if you just told him someone was here to see him."

Carol Howard looked at him for a couple of beats.

"Do I need to be scared?"

"No, Ms. Howard," Evan said quietly. "You don't need to be frightened."

She nodded, gestured at the sofa and loveseat in a general way, then went down a hallway to the right. Evan and Goff remained standing. She came back a moment later. "He's coming."

"Thank you," Evan said.

"Thank you, ma'am," Goff added with a nod.

"I'm going to go back to Mrs. Draper now."

"That'll be fine, Ms. Howard," Evan told her.

She hesitated for a second, then went down another hallway to the left. Evan heard a door shut quietly. Just a few seconds later, Brian Draper walked into the living room.

He was about fifty, a little overweight, not bad looking, but ordinary. He was wearing a checked shirt, cargo shorts, and a quizzical expression.

"Can I help you?" he asked.

"Mr. Draper?" Evan asked.

"Yes."

Evan held out his hand. "Hello. I'm Sheriff Evan Caldwell, and this is Sgt. Ruben Goff."

The man took Evan's hand, but while he conceded to a shake, he didn't exactly shake back.

"Hello," he said.

"Do you mind if we all sit down, Mr. Draper?"

"I guess not, but what is this about?"

"Let's sit down and talk a minute," Evan said.

Draper sat down on the sofa that was right behind him. Evan and Goff sat on the loveseat, and Evan held a hand out to Goff, who handed him the file. Evan opened it. He noticed that Draper's gaze was fixed on the folder.

"Mr. Draper, you're the stepson of Daniel Miner, is that right?" Evan asked.

"That's right," the man said to the file.

"Is he here?"

"No. Uh…no. He passed away over a year ago."

"I see. How did he die?"

"He, uh, he was ill anyway, he'd had a stroke. But he died of a heart attack."

"Where was he interred?"

"What?"

"Is he buried here, or is he in a military cemetery, or what? He was a vet, right?"

"Vietnam," the man answered quietly. "He wanted to have his ashes spread at sea. So, we did that."

"I see. Where was he cremated?"

Draper was starting to look pretty uncomfortable. "I can't remember the name of the place."

"I see. When did he pass away again?"

"February before last," the man answered.

"So who's been cashing his checks?" Evan asked.

It took a moment. "What?" Draper finally asked.

"His pension from the phone company and his social security," Evan answered. "They've all been deposited into an account held by your mother and stepfather, right up to the first and third of this month."

Draper was looking a little pale. His eyes were twitching.

"You've been depositing his checks," Evan said for him. "Through the bank's mobile app."

"Uh…no, I—"

"Did you kill your stepfather to get that money?"

"What? No!"

"Then how is it that there is no death certificate on record for your stepfather, nor is there any record of him having been buried or cremated by any of the five funeral homes in this county?"

"I don't know!"

"Did you perhaps bury him in a residential development called Seaview Cove?"

The man started shaking his head. "No."

Evan pulled an xray from the folder and placed it on the oak coffee table between them. That's an xray of your stepfather's spine. We got it from the VA." He slid another xray onto the table. "And that's the spine of a man found buried in the front yard of an as-yet uncompleted house. As you can see, both of them have the exact same bit of shrapnel lodged near the lower spine. Did you know your stepfather had been injured in Vietnam?"

"I knew he was there. I knew he got hurt and was sent home," the man said. "He didn't really talk about it."

"So, since you say his ashes were spread at sea, but this and a pair of fingerprints from the victim we found both say he was Daniel Miner, how do you explain that?"

The man sat there, staring at Evan.

"Did you kill your stepfather and bury him across town?" Evan asked.

"No! No, I didn't!" The man started blinking rapidly. "He had a heart attack, like I said."

"There's no death certificate for Daniel Miner, Mr. Draper."

The man rubbed at his face. "No. I know." He blinked some more. "But I didn't do anything to him. He just had a heart attack, right on the back porch."

"But you wanted the checks to keep coming," Evan said.

Draper let out a huge breath. "I didn't…I just—yes, I buried him. Yes, I took the checks," he said. "But it's not what you think. I'm not a bad person."

"Explain it to us."

"My mother needs constant care," he said. "She has dementia. Her insurance won't cover full-time home health care. Medicaid won't cover it, but they won't cover a nursing home, either. Not all of it, and I don't have it."

Evan waited for him to go on.

"If I stayed home with her, who would pay the mortgage? Who would pay the bills?"

"Doesn't your mother get VA benefits from your stepfather's service?" Evan asked.

Draper opened his mouth but shut it again without saying anything. Evan stood, and Goff followed suit.

"Mr. Draper, I'm going to have to place you under arrest, and you'll be coming with us."

"I didn't kill him! He died right out back, sitting on a patio chair!"

Evan didn't know whether Draper had killed his stepfather or not. Ebersole was still waiting on toxicology and further testing of the man's ruined organs.

"Sir, at the very least, you've committed several felonies, including fraud and the illegal interment of a body. We're working on the rest."

"I need to call a lawyer," the man said.

"You'll be given that opportunity."

# TWENTY-TWO

THE FOLLOWING MORNING, Evan arrived at the station early, but not before Vi. Never before Vi. She offered a "Good morning, Mr. Caldwell" that sounded more like a warning than a greeting.

Evan just smiled and asked if Vi had heard from Paula yet this morning.

"I have a note from her, from last night," Vi said, peering over her bifocals at the monitor. "It says that she doesn't need an assistant that bad. It should be 'badly' of course, but it says 'bad'. I assume you know what she's talking about?"

"I showed Holland the evidence photos from Grundy's," Evan said. "I was trying to offer an olive branch, show him some respect in hopes of a like gesture on his part."

"And you thought since he'd already seen the secret evidence, he could help Paula process it."

"Sure," Evan said. "Two birds and all that."

Vi gave him a long look, over the top of her glasses. It wasn't exactly an accusatory stare, more contemplative, but the longer she looked at him, the dumber he felt.

Vi's computer beeped, and she let her eyes travel back to it. She tapped a few keys, shuffled a couple of papers, and in general, seemed to have returned to whatever it was she was doing before Evan arrived.

Just about the time he figured on moving through to his own office, Vi said, without turning from her screen, "The longer you keep those boxes sealed, the bigger they'll get."

Evan stopped, his hand on the door to his office. "What have you heard?"

"At my age, I've heard just about everything," Vi said, turning again to look at him. "As far as Grundy and his secret boxes, I've heard anything from women's underwear to eyeballs in formaldehyde, but the general consensus is that the good doctor either had a collection of hearts in jars, or possibly brains."

"Brains?"

Vi nodded once. The chains dangling from her glasses swung in echo of that nod. "It is certainly not my place to tell you your business, Mr. Caldwell, but with the way rumors have of growing, in another day or two, anything less than brains will be a major disappointment."

"I see," Evan said.

Vi turned back to her computer. "Paula just pulled in around back; did you need something from her?"

The station's video surveillance feeds were available on the computer network. Evan knew Vi frequently had those feeds scrolling across the bottom of her monitor. He assumed this was how she knew Paula had arrived. Though he didn't rule out omniscience.

"I do," he said. "I need to take her back out to Grundy's this morning, first thing. Can you ask Goff to run muster this morning?'

Vi nodded, "I'm sure he'll be thrilled."

Evan collected Danny's report and the scene photos from his office, then went and collected Paula from her lab. She wasn't amenable to being collected, but after eyeing the boxes, decided that a field trip to Grundy's house would be a better way to start the morning. She followed Evan, in her own car, to the scene.

Once they got to Grundy's, Evan got out, opened the back driver's-side door, and lifted out the evidence box he'd borrowed. In it were a cheap new bowling ball the same weight as Grundy's, a silver water bottle that would stand in for a flask, a magazine, some shoelaces, and a towel that he'd picked up at Dick's Sporting

Goods. There was also a tote he'd grabbed at The Pig on his way to work.

"Let's go," he told Paula as she approached the Pilot.

Paula followed him up the ramp and through the sliding door once he'd gotten it open. They stepped around the dried stains in front of the closet, remnants of the fluids that begin to leak from a decomposing body.

Paula followed Evan to the closest kitchen counter, where he set down the box. He set the folder with the scene photos and Danny's report aside and lifted the lid. Paula raised her eyebrows when he lifted out the bowling ball.

"You planning on taking me bowling later?" Paula asked him. Evan just smiled at her as he put everything from the box into the tote. "I can't say I appreciate being your second choice after Holland."

"Listen," Evan said. "I asked him out here because he knew a little bit about Grundy outside of the job. He told me something yesterday, but I was too busy enjoying his company and I missed it until sometime late last night."

"I'll try not to entertain to the point of distraction. What did he say?"

"Come over here by the closet," Evan said, tote in one hand and file in the other.

Paula joined him in the laundry room. "So, what are we looking at?"

"I know you've only gotten partway through processing the materials you collected here, but is there any evidence at all that there was another person inside the house at the time Grundy died?"

Paula shook her head. "Not at the time he died. Not at all. The only prints we got were Grundy's, but I wouldn't have had company over, either. All of the hairs, fibers, and prints I've looked at all come back to Grundy."

"Right," Evan nodded. "So, we originally thought someone came to his back door and assaulted him here. Except, there is nothing on the sliding door to indicate he had a visitor ..."

"Grundy's were the only prints on the handle or the glass. We might try to find trace DNA on the upper portion of the door or door frame if somebody knocked, but that's pretty iffy." She eyed him, curiously. "So no one inside, no one at the sliding door. What are you thinking?"

"I'm thinking Grundy caved his own head in."

# TWENTY-THREE

EVAN HANDED PAULA the file, and she opened it. "How tall was Grundy?" he asked.

Paula opened the binder and flipped a couple pages. "Five-three."

"Okay." He opened the hall closet. The sliding door was already open. "This is about how we found it, correct?"

Paula flipped a few more pages, consulted a photo she found there, then stepped forward, adjusting the closet door minutely. "More like that."

Evan looked at her photos, then back up at the door. "Right. Now look in the closet; the top shelf."

Paula looked up, flipped to a photo she had taken of the open closet, examined it, then she looked back up at the shelf. "You're looking at the gap on the top shelf?"

"Yes."

On the right side of the shelf sat a stack of hat boxes. Paula had already checked them to find they contained only hats. On the left was an old plastic box marked Hurricane Survival Kit, which held a flashlight and transistor radio, corroded batteries and a few bottles of (now dehydrated) water. These items had enough dust to suggest they may have been there since the house belonged to the elderly couple under the wheelchair ramp. But between these was a gap about a foot wide, where no dust had settled.

"We decided that's probably where he kept his Piggly Wiggly," Paula said, nodding at Evan's bag.

"Right," Evan said. "And yesterday, Holland told me that Grundy always carried his ball in this bag."

Paula's eyes widened, and a disbelieving grin creased one side of her face. She gave a half snort, half laugh. "No fricken way."

"Grundy's five-three," Evan said. "The shelf is almost six-six. His ball is a 14-pounder. Physics. Very smooth surface on the weapon, a great deal of force. But not a swing, just gravity."

Paula was shaking her head, flipping back and forth between a couple different photos, looking from shelf to floor to photos to door. She laughed again, then covered her mouth, and muttered, "Crap," through her fingers. "You think he somehow dropped the ball on his own head, like it rolled out of the bag, bounced off his head, and then out the door?"

"He staggered a step or two back, against the wall, and then went down," Evan stepped aside and pointed at the stains. "By then the ball was out the door."

Evan crooked his finger at her and she followed him out onto the ramp. "The ball rolled down the ramp, down the driveway, and picked up enough momentum to carry it all the way over there."

Evan pointed at the access road and the Dinkelman lot.

"Where a bunch of kids found it the next night."

"I wish we could have determined his BAC," Paula said. "Might make this scenario a bit easier to swallow."

"I doubt anyone's going to believe he was sober at six-thirty on a Friday night," Evan said.

"That's a pretty precise time of death. How'd you come up with that?"

"He was going bowling," Evan said. "His pals expected him at seven and it takes a little over half an hour to get there from here, and Grundy's always late."

Paula laughed again, pulled a pen from her shirt pocket and started writing notes in the back of the file folder. "You want me to go over this again, take some measurements, see if I can get any hard evidence to confirm?"

"If it's not too much trouble."

"If this isn't a murder investigation, do we still need to process those dolls as part of a crime scene?"

"Not a crime scene if it's accidental. The dolls wouldn't be part of a death investigation."

"Then it's no trouble at all," Paula said. Now her grin was significantly less cynical. "I'll get my kit and see if your theory fits the facts."

She headed for her car then paused and turned back to him. "What are you going to do with the stuff we collected?"

"They're evidence removed from the scene of an accident. They'll collect dust in the lockup for the requisite number of years, and then they'll probably be incinerated."

"Problem solved?"

"Mitigated," Evan said. "We might still need to talk to the families. And I'll give a statement to the press, de-sensationalize it, and hope some other scandal comes up over in Franklin County so we can get on with our lives."

He withdrew his cigarettes and started to shake one out of the pack.

"I'd appreciate it if you'd not do that," Paula said.

"Thought you took a break from quitting."

"I did," she said. "Break's over."

Evan smiled. "Good for you."

He slipped the pack back into his pocket. "You're my hero and all."

As he walked down the wheelchair ramp, he heard Paula humming "On Top of Old Smoky." At first, he thought she was referring to his habit. But then he started laughing.

# TWENTY-FOUR

THE FOLLOWING SATURDAY morning, Evan was enjoying the last of his scrambled egg sandwich at the Dockside Grill. It was a beautiful day; cooler than it had been. More like April and Evan was in a good mood.

Evan flicked the possibility of crumbs from his blue button-down and his khakis. The gulls collected on the pilings across the dock took notice. He tossed the last of his bread to the dock, and they all went at it at once, too busy screeching to actually snatch it up.

Above their chatter, mast riggings clinked as all of the sailboats rocked in the gentle breeze.

Beneath all these sounds, yet somehow distinctly audible, Evan heard the *tac, tac, tac* of Abby's heels stomping toward him, as delicately as heels can stomp. When she reached the chair opposite him, she just stood there, not smiling.

He gave her the opportunity to speak first, but, when she declined, Evan said, "It's a good deal, Abby. The best he could have hoped for."

"Of course, it is," she snapped, "An offer I can't refuse."

"I'm glad to have found some common ground," Evan said.

"Thirty years?" she asked, dropping her folder on his table and plopping into the chair across from him.

"With the possibility of parole, good behavior and all that. He'll have a chance to get an education on the inside, a chance at a bit of a real life after."

Abby glared at him.

"Best of all," Evan said, leaning forward, "He gets to stop being everybody's pawn."

"What if we say 'no'?"

"You know what will happen. DA Chimes will let it be known that Nathan Beckett caused a bit of a warrant and search and seizure mess. The judge will remove you as council and get Tommy a competent lawyer. If somebody happens to pass him the file you gave me, *somebody* might even get disbarred."

"Defense attorneys conduct surveillance all the time; you know that."

"Of suspects, not the sheriff on his day off." Evan wiped his mouth with his napkin, then put it on his plate. "For what it's worth," Evan said, "Chimes is just about as furious as you are. He tossed out a perfectly good murder case this morning, just for spite."

Abby's glare softened, or at least the daggers lost their edge. "Wait, what murder case? Grundy?"

"No, turns out Grundy dropped a bowling ball on his own head," Evan said. "I'm talking about the body we found at Seaview. He was a Purple Heart veteran of Vietnam, a guy named Daniel Miner. The stepson confessed to burying him there but claims he died of 'old age.' Autopsy and Miner's doc say probably not, but they're still working on that. But Chimes won't roll on it."

"Serves you right," Abby said.

"I'm okay with it. At the very least, he's going for a heap of fraud charges, one for every check he deposited. Possibly manslaughter as well. And his mother's getting the care she would have gotten anyway, from the VA."

"What's a girl got to do to get a cup of coffee around here?"

"I got it," Evan said, flagging a waitress.

"Least you could do," she muttered. "Why won't he take your case? The official version?"

"I'm not going to repeat his exact words in mixed company," Evan said, "Wouldn't want to offend your delicate sensibilities, but I think the real reason is he's afraid of you."

Abby's eyebrows raised. The glint in her eye told Evan that however down she felt about losing the opportunity to take the Morrow case to trial, it was only a temporary condition.

"The stepson's story was that he hid the body so he could keep getting Miner's pension and SSI because his mother needs round the clock medical care," Evan said. "Chimes is afraid that you could turn that into another sob story to beat him over the head with."

Abby laughed out loud, startling the waitress who was just in the process of serving her the coffee. A bit of the coffee slopped across the tablecloth. The waitress apologized and scurried away. Abby noticed none of this.

"He's right!" she said, smiling. At one time, Evan had thought her smile was kind of pretty. Now he found all of her ugly. "I would have raked his sorry butt over the coals from one end of that courtroom to the other. Poor guy's just trying to take care of his mom."

"The VA would have taken care of her, either way," Evan said.

"Sure, they would...and still will," Abby said. "But, here's the fun part, Sheriff. What do you think is going to happen next time Chimes tries to bring a murder case? I'm going to beat his ass on the news for letting a murderer walk free." She immediately switched personas, taking on the melodramatically appalled role of a TV lawyer. "What kind of District Attorney lets a Vietnam vet get murdered and lets the killer walk?"

Evan had to laugh, "He's not going to walk."

"He just better hope I don't pull that case," she said. After a pause, she added, "I'm still going to run, you know." It sounded like a challenge.

"I hope you do," Evan said. "I'd rather deal with you as a councilperson than as public defender."

"I'm not sure if that's a compliment," she said, as Evan stood.

"It isn't."

# TWENTY-FIVE

EVAN AND SARAH walked to the runabout, which was tied up behind the Chris-Craft. Evan had an empty backpack slung over his shoulder. He took the cooler from Sarah, then handed her aboard before jumping down into the boat.

As Sarah loosed the stern line, Evan ran through his mental checklist for getting underway. Once he'd started the engine, he looked up at the swim platform on the back of the Chris-Craft.

Plutes sat there twitching his tail, looking at Evan like Evan had something hanging out of his nose.

"Are you coming, or what?" Evan snapped at him.

Sarah laughed and sat down on one of the deck boxes. "You want me to lure him with one of the tuna fish sandwiches?"

"He doesn't need luring; he just needs to move his fat black behind." He looked back at Plutes, gunning the throttle just a hair. "I'm perfectly happy to go out on the bay without every one of your twenty toenails sticking into my back. So, if you want to go surfing today, you need to come aboard. Otherwise, try not to piss on anything while I'm gone."

Plutes blinked, switched his tail once, then jumped first to the bow and then over the windscreen. Then he jumped over to Sarah's deck box. Evan slid the backpack over his shoulders.

"Cram him on in here," he said.

Sarah lifted the cat, who didn't growl when *she* did it, then gently put him into the backpack.

Evan sighed as Plutes shifted this way and that, finally digging at least ten scythe-like claws into Evan's back and poking his head out the open top.

"He needs to get a grip and learn how to use that halter," Evan said over the engine.

He took care of the bowline, reversed, and pulled out around the stern of the Chris-Craft. Sarah appeared beside him as he crept through the remainder of the no-wake zone, thankful that his was the closest slip to the channel.

"You know that people who aren't cat people don't actually take their cats surfing, right?"

"I don't know anything at all about cat people."

"They don't."

"I'm just trying to make him a little bit more bearable to deal with," Evan said.

"That's what little balls and catnip are for," Sarah said.

"Catnip makes him moan like a teenaged girl at Woodstock," Evan said. "I almost threw him overboard."

Sarah smiled, then shut her yap while they moved out of the no-wake and sped up, headed for the channel.

"It's so cute the way his lips curl back like that when you get going," Sarah said, raising her voice a bit.

"Sure," Evan replied.

"You know he's *your* cat, right?"

"That's what you think," Evan snapped. "What do you think we're using for bait today?"

Sarah shook her head, and Evan looked over his shoulder as she went back to the deck box and sat down. He shook his head, then faced forward again.

Once they were well out onto Saint Joseph Bay, Evan gave it a little more throttle. As he did, he felt a vibration between his shoulder blades. After a moment, he determined that, yes, the idiot was actually purring.

"Shut up," Evan said.

## THE END

Read on for links to the other books in the *Still Waters Suspense Series*, and to find out how to get all new releases at a discount. Thanks so much for reading, and we hope you had some fun!

# THANK YOU FOR READING
# DEAD AND GONE

WE HOPE YOU had fun with the third book in the Still Waters Suspense series. If you missed the first book, *Dead Reckoning*, you can find it here:

AMAZON.COM/DP/B075FL22C9

To get a heads-up for each new release, and to find out about discounts, free books, and public appearances, you can sign up for the mailing list here:

DAWNLEEMCKENNA.COM

You might also enjoy Dawn Lee McKenna's original series, the Forgotten Coast Florida Suspense series, which is set in Apalachicola, FL, and which introduces the character of Evan Caldwell. You can find that series, as well as Dawn Lee's Southern fiction novel, See You, here:

AMAZON.COM/GP/PRODUCT/B079DTTWH2

All are available on Kindle Unlimited.

If you are interested in something a little out of the mainstream, have a look at Axel Blackwell's paranormal thrillers here.

AMAZON.COM/AXEL-BLACKWELL/E/B00W0I2UO4

You can also visit the Dawn Lee McKenna Facebook page, where you'll find pictures of locations and people used in both series, updates on new books, news about author events, and a lot of odd people, including Dawn Lee.

FB.COM/DAWN-LEE-MCKEN-NA-1470505269903994/

# ABOUT THE
# AUTHORS

DAWN LEE MCKENNA is the author of the novel
*See You*, and the bestselling *Forgotten Coast Florida Suspense*
series. A native of Florida, she now lives in northeastern
Tennessee with her five children and one domineering cat.

AXEL BLACKWELL GREW up in one of those
small Indiana towns where the only fun is the kind you
make yourself. Many ghost and UFO sightings in central
Indiana between 1985 and 1990 can be attributed to
Axel and his brothers attempting to escape boredom.
Axel now lives with his family and an assortment of
animals in the Pacific Northwest.

CPSIA information can be obtained
at www.ICGtesting.com
Printed in the USA
LVHW011128251019
635331LV00007B/140/P

9 780998 666969